Hades and Persephone

Keeper of Sins

Gods of Myth
Book One

ALANNAH CARBONNEAU

Cover Image Art @ Depositphoto

Proofreading by Virginia Test Carey

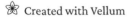 Created with Vellum

This is for you.
For the reader who needs just a little bit of myth.
A dash of magic.
And a pinch of spice.

Enjoy!

DEAR READERS

I've always been immensely fascinated by Greek Mythology, but the story of Hades and Persephone has captivated me like no other. Because of this, I decided it was time to write my own spin on their story.

Although I adore Greek Myth, this book is a work of fiction, and therefore I have taken liberties with this story and the characters within. The following does not represent my own views on religion/God/Gods. This is purely fiction and meant for entertainment purposes only.

Keeping the above in mind, I do hope that you find as much enjoyment in reading this book as I have found in writing it.

As always, enjoy, and thank you for reading and supporting my work.

CHAPTER
ONE

P *ersephone*

"PERSEPHONE!" Like it has so many times before, the voice pulls me violently from sleep. It's an animal sound, my name in the roar of desperate rage. Beneath the anger, there is an echo of something more. A symphony of ancient anguish.

It cools my blood, pebbling my flesh with unease.

I've been waking to the call of a man no one else can hear my entire life. As far back as I can remember, I can recall the pain of his rough, unchanging anguish. The soul-deep rage that clings to the pain—too deep for me to possibly explore.

Too deep for anyone to explore. I can't even

imagine an ocean trench being vast enough to encompass the breadth of his sorrow. His torment is a tortured melody that tears me from sleep, and more recently, interrupts even my waking moments.

There was once a time, when I was too young to know better, that I would ask others if they heard him. My Sunday school teacher had guffawed in horror, clutching the gold cross around her neck. Mom and Dad had hushed me, explaining it all away with excuses or calls for attention. Until the calls became too frequent, and I started seeing the doctors. Even as a child, I could see something in the doctor's eyes when he asked me about the voice I heard. He pressed to know if this voice told me to do things. Bad things. He pressed for my most secret and shameful thoughts. Only, I didn't have any.

My thoughts regarding the voice even then had been worry. A sorrowful fear that another was hurting beyond comprehension. A sense that I alone could see to that hurt. Could make it better. Could ease it, if just a bit.

During my visits with the doctor, Mom and Dad would wait. Mom's nails were always bitten to the bed, her knees jumping anxiously. Dad's head was always bowed between his shoulders, as though he carried a weight too massive to bear. It didn't take me long to learn that what I heard was not normal. It was not normal in a way that would eventually bear a terrible kind of consequence I did not want to have to pay.

Deep in the night, when the voice would wake me and I'd creep from my room to Mom and Dad's for comfort, I'd heard their hushed arguments. They whispered of mental illness, of disease, and a life of hospitals.

Dad spoke of barbaric treatments. Mom spoke of prayer. They feared something was deeply wrong with me. Something terrifying and shameful.

I was a test from God, or a curse from the devil.

Their marriage was cracking. Because of me.

I learned in those early moments that I could not share this pain I felt in the depths of me. I could not share the man's anguished cry of my name. Not with the doctors, the church, or even with my parents.

I could not confide in the two people I should have been able to trust wholly and without restriction.

I terrified them.

At the tender age of seven, I learned to keep the voice to myself. I stopped telling them of how I woke in the night. I denied hearing the voice when asked. The doctor gloated in pleasure when he diagnosed me with an imaginary friend, not unlike many other children. He claimed my parents had no need to worry, and they eagerly believed him.

My Sunday school teacher sighed in relief at the news, but never quite looked at me as she did the other kids.

I learned what normal looked like and replicated it to please those around me. For years, it worked. I think it's still working.

I attended school, and worked hard to top the honor roll. I danced and played sports. I tended the farm with Dad, and worked with Mom in town in her flower shop. I sat between them in the pew every Sunday, my mind far, far away.

I grew a soul-deep love of art; paintings in specific. Though I had no ability with the brush, my appreciation for art never waned. Nor did it grow spite in the yawning shadow that is my lack of talent. I looked at a brushstroke and felt somehow closer to the voice that called my name in my mind. To the unexplained agony that festered in the depths of my soul.

Beneath the night sky, under the white shadow of a full-bellied moon, I felt alive. Staring into a golden flame, I burned with desire I could not name. And I'd been entirely obsessed with all things Greek Mythology, since I studied Ancient Greece in grade six. The Gods and Goddesses fascinated me to no end, even though Mom was always quick to tell me the myths were nothing more than stories, and there was only one God. Our God.

Still, the bookshelves in my room were bursting with texts and stories about the Gods and Goddesses. Maybe it was my name, Persephone, that drew me to the myths. I was captivated by the stories of Hades' claiming of his queen. The cruelty in the capture of a young girl. The deceit woven into the fabric of an unwanted love. The centuries and centuries—*the millennia*—of hateful spite that followed in the aftermath as a Goddess—a mother, scorned by the loss of her daughter to the God of the Underworld, starved the earth for six months of the year in what the people would begin to call the *seasons*.

I'd once asked Mom why she named me Persephone, and she had told me she'd liked the name Stephanie, but it was too common. She'd read the name Persephone in a book, and it had resonated. And that was how I'd become Persephone. Funny how, now, everyone calls me Annie.

I haven't been called *Persephone* outside of the man who roars my name in my mind. I haven't heard my name outside of my dreams, in ages.

Mom's hands come to either side of my face, and she leans in to press her warm lips to my forehead. Behind her, Dad's scruffy jaw is hard.

He doesn't want me to go. He's been vocal about this, unusually hostile, even.

For the most part, Dad is a teddy bear in blue jeans, plaid, and dirt-caked fingernails. But he's always been somewhat unreceptive when it came to my obsession with Greek Mythology. He's only little more receptive of my fascination with art, and slightly more so of the degree in archeology I aspire to work toward, specializing, of course, in the Hellenic Republic.

He's proud of the fact I want to go to school. That I have the desire to nourish my mind and enrich my life with a sustainable career. Even though he doesn't love the fact archaeology in itself will take me away from home more often than I'd be there, I know he's proud.

What he doesn't love is that I'm aspiring, specifically, to study archaeology *in* Greece. If it weren't so difficult to find jobs within the art sector, I know he'd be waving that flag high and wide. Alas, a career in art is not easy, and the theory of the starving artist has left him with a sour taste on his tongue.

I know what he's hoping. He's hoping that I'll go to Greece and explore enough of the country under the safety of a very expensive four-month programme in which I will be introduced to the career I think I so desperately want—and hate it. He's hoping for itchy bug bites and sunburns and heat stroke. Nothing too harmful, of course, but an in general awful experience that will have me tucking tail and returning home.

He'd been so opposed to the idea of my summer in Greece, that after a lifetime of promises to aid me in my education, he'd flatly refused to invest in *this*.

So, I'd dumped nearly my entire life savings from working nights in Mom's flower shop into this experience. It left me with very little to see myself through the next four months in Greece. I will no doubt have to find a job, but that's fine. That's totally fine.

It only adds to the experience, right?

"You call as soon as you land," Mom demands, and

Dad gives me a firm nod. The only thing he's agreed to continue paying for is my cell phone, and the unlimited international minutes I'll need to keep in daily contact with home.

"I will."

Mom sniffles. "And make sure you wear a hat every day." Her lips pull down in a pouty frown. "You're so fair, you're going to come back looking like crisped bacon."

I don't tell her she's being dramatic, even though she is. "I'll wear my hat." I hurry to add when she opens her mouth, "And sunscreen."

I hate sunscreen, but I wear it always. For Mom.

Her mouth clamps closed and with a slightly narrowed eye, and a cheeky grin Dad misses, she leans in to press a second kiss to my forehead. "I love you, Annie."

"I love you, too." I step from her embrace to Dad's. He instantly wraps me in his bear hug. It's the one I recall from my youth. The one that never changed, remaining constant always in a world that is ever-shifting.

"Love you, kiddo," he murmurs gruffly into my fair hair. Emotion thickens his usually smooth voice, and his hug tightens, kiss deepening in my nearly white locks.

I have no idea where I got it, because both Mom and Dad have muddy-toned, brown hair. Mine is so blonde, it's touching albino white. At least I have

Dad's green eyes and Mom's full, pink lips. I might not share her hair color, but I did inherit her fall of uniform, smooth waves.

I know I'm theirs, not adopted. Despite my fair hair, I look too much like them to question the validity of my bloodline. I think, if I'd been adopted, they'd have found some way to return me for the stress I'd put them under as a young child facing a potential personality diagnosis of some sort or another.

But we don't talk about the voice. We never talk about the voice. It's like it never happened. Never was.

I haven't told a soul about the fact I still hear him. Or that I hear him more often now than ever before. His calls for me growing more and more frequent, more insistent. The enraged anguish tugging the threads of my soul away from this place to another, far, far away land.

Sometimes, in the moments I'm struck by his call, stripped of sanity in the aftermath of my need to seek a way to respond to him, I think it's why I'm going to Greece.

And that terrifies me.

Because if I'm following a voice no one else hears across the globe—then maybe I really am insane.

TWO

P *ersephone*

THE FIRST THING I notice upon arriving in Greece is the scent of salty, somehow sandy, heat. You might think you can't smell heat, but you can. There is a wafting plume of it that rises from the ancient stone land, swirling in the air from the creamy, sometimes shockingly white, buildings and cobbled stone. Under the heat, or maybe enriched by it, is the scent of fresh herbs.

Originally from Canada, and an Alberta farm girl at that, the city feels incredibly, hypnotically old. It's nothing like the young country that birthed me, and yet, nowhere I've ever travelled has ever felt so much like coming home.

I inhale another big breath of heat and herbs deep into my lungs, and sigh. My body hums under the high, hot sun. My soul titters. Yes, my *soul* titters.

It's like nothing I've ever experienced, my arrival into this country. This ancient place. I have yet to explore. To sink my hands into the earth or my feet into the sea. And yet I've never felt a sense of belonging such as this.

This place, this country, it is where my soul is meant to rest.

It's a bizarre thought for a woman of nineteen to entertain. The resting place of my soul should have no bearing on my youthful desires. Yet the thought is there in the forefront of my mind. A realization I can't deny.

Maybe it's the old soul that burns inside me. The soul Grammy always said was too wise, too guarded to have lived just this one life.

My old soul recognizes this place. With every deep, salty breath. In every blade of sand, there is recognition in the great fabric of the ethereal design that weaves me.

I was meant for this place. I *am* meant for this place.

～

I FLOP down on the narrow, too hard bed, and loose a sigh from the deep of my belly. I'm still wearing the broad brimmed straw hat that I wear during my days in the sun. The buttons of my light, billowy blue and white striped long sleeve shirt are undone to display the white tank I wear underneath. I've been here for a week. I've explored what a career might mean in archaeology during the day under the blistering, delicious sun. And at night I've explored the city, called to it like a moth to flame.

I've enjoyed authentic food and trapsed through the most adorable shops that line winding, narrow roads. I've stopped to talk to people, engaging for hours in conversation about this great city, the ancient history, and the lore that remains today. Every day, I've fallen a little more in love. I honestly don't know how I'll ever go home again.

Home doesn't feel like home anymore.

"You should stay in tonight." My roommate throws me a mocking smile. "Get some sleep."

With a groan and quite possibly a rattle of my bones, I roll to my side. Flicking off my hat, I prop my head on a fist and give Willa a look.

She laughs. "Okay, okay, since you're *not* willing to sleep, you should come out with us."

I'd heard the chatter about tonight while engaged in examining newly discovered artifacts with my supervisor at the Eleusis site. Everything I touched, everything I saw, it all felt oddly familiar. Like triggering a memory from a time I couldn't possibly have lived.

The longer I'm here, the more potent my madness feels. The louder the call of his pained cry echoes in my mind.

The longer I am here, the more I feel I know this place. These ancient things lost to the earth and buried by time.

Only today I touched a stone swept clean of sand. There are theories that the rubble of the once illustrious temple belonged to Hades, God of the Dead. But when I touched the stone with my naked fingertips, my gloves discarded, heart pounding, I'd been assaulted by visions of a time I could not possibly know. A woman kneeling in respect to Demeter, Goddess of Harvest and Agriculture, before she was given a grain of wheat.

I'd pulled my hand back, severing the vision along with my touch. Inside my heart, a spear of pain had me gasping in shock. I felt—*I ached* at the thought of the Goddess. A betrayal unlike any I've ever known. Unlike anything I could imagine. It swept through my veins like a violent and terrible tsunami, threatening to wash all of me away.

Hesitantly, I'd touched the stone a second time to experience only the sensation of sunbaked sandstone centuries old and assaulted by time.

I'd excused it all away the same way Mom excuses my oddities. *It's my overactive imagination.*

I clear my throat, giving my head a shake as I refocus on Willa. "You mean the club?"

"Yeah, The Tower of Pluto. It's not far from here."

"I've seen it." It's hard not to when it lights up the night sky. Its show-stopping ring of fire at the cloud-scraping top ignites the city in a blazing glow of red embers. They spark and fall like stars dipped in blood against an obsidian night, winking out before they ever connect with the ground.

I've caught myself making wishes on those falling embers as one might wish upon a star.

Willa tosses the small closet wide. "I've heard it's owned by a man named Hades Pluton."

I snort, my eyes snapping wide. "Seriously?"

Willa giggles, as knowledgeable in Greek Myth as me. "Right? His parents must have hated him." Her nose wrinkles. "Or maybe they were just goofy people, and they didn't mind their son being the butt of a crappy joke for the rest of his life."

I shrug. "At least he made something of his name, I guess."

I mean, the guy clearly used it well, what with the Tower of Pluto. In a city of white stone and blue topped roofs, the bleached stone Tower of Pluto is veined in black obsidian that abducts the sun's prisms every day, and a torched top that sears the stars at night. It's a clever mockery of the untouchable *Olympus*, I can't help but think, scorched by hellfire. Or, more accurately, the fires of Tartarus.

"Apparently, he lives in the top of the tower, and, like, never leaves," Willa continues. "He's an artist—a painter—and it's said one should never visit Athens without also visiting the Tower of Pluto. His art is displayed on the walls, never for sale, so it's the only place you can see it." She pulls a dress from the closet. "Apparently, Hades takes *tortured artist* to a whole new level."

"With a name like his, I can see why that might be," I say, but my interest is piqued. I've never been one for clubbing, and outside of sharing a glass of wine with Mom over the holidays, I don't drink. But art—art is something I have an incredibly hard time refusing. "When are you leaving?"

"A couple hours," Willa says, holding a black dress up to her body in the mirror.

"Good." I push up from the bed. "I have time to shower."

THREE

P *ersephone*

"DAMN, girl, you're like the friggin' poster child for tits and ass." Claire's lips twist to the side in a half-pout, half look of disgust that has me feeling far more self-conscious than I like.

"It's that bad?"

Willa shoots a jab into my ribs with her elbow as I'm trying to tug at the hem of Willa's short dress I wear. I hadn't packed anything for clubbing, because I'm not the kind of girl who clubs. Mom would pitch a fit, running straight for Pastor Tanner. The same pastor who'd once prayed the devil from my young soul.

Dad would—well, he'd just give me those disappointed eyes. The ones that accompany the thinning of tight lips before a slow head nod of disapproving acceptance.

"Stop tugging," Willa commands. "It's not bad. You look hot."

Claire's eyes do another sweep, and she heaves a sigh. "She's right. You're stupid hot!" Under her breath, but with a teasing smile, she adds, "Bitch."

I don't understand Claire. She's the wild one, always shooting flirty smiles to all the boys. And they're there for it, gobbling up everything she serves like they're lost in the desert and she's water. I wonder when they'll realize she's a cactus, and they're going to get poked far before they get a taste.

"Holy crap!" Claire's jaw drops, spreading glossy lips wide. "Look at the line."

Willa stops, shoulders falling. "Shit."

I look between the two of them. "What? This isn't normal?"

Claire tears her eyes from the line that weaves up and down the street and into a torch-lit alley. "You think this is normal? Where are you from?"

"Alberta."

Claire's brows knit. "Where?"

"Canada," Willa answers for me, but she sounds direly bored. "She's a farm girl from an itty-bitty town. Is it even a town or one of those hamlet things? Never mind," she brushes off before I can answer. "I don't think she's ever been clubbing."

"Never!" Claire's eyes are big. She's being over-dramatic.

There are tons of people who choose not to club. Not to imbibe and strip themselves of all inhibitions in the name of a good time only to wake cloaked in regrets. I know a whole *town* of them, in fact. Okay, maybe it's a Hamlet. Whatever.

"Nope." I sigh, because this is already feeling like it's going to be a long night. I don't fit in with Claire. Willa, either, if I'm being honest. Though, at least I can talk to Willa.

Relationships with people my age have always felt stilted. They never come naturally, but I am trying. I promised myself on the plane that I would try.

I just wish it was easier. Not so forced. So awkward and stilted.

"That's wild." Claire's eyes dance wickedly. "We're going to get you so drunk."

Willa smirks at my nervous laugh as we settle at the end of a very, very long line. I'm already feeling the weight of exhaustion ten minutes later. I'm not accustomed to wearing heels. I don't even wear heels to church on Sunday. I'm a jeans, leggings, and sneakers kind of girl. In the summer, you can't find me in socks. I default to flip flops and sandals. I'm low-key, so these sky-high fire-red heels are beyond out of place for me.

The white slouchy dress is another matter entirely.

It's far too short for comfort. *There's no way I'm dancing tonight.*

And it's backless. The fabric hangs from my shoulders in a sweeping fall to the small of my back. Because it's backless, Willa had insisted I go braless. Braless with D cups isn't practical, *at all.*

I don't know what I'm doing here, with these girls.

I'm not this girl.

I'm so out of place.

My anxiety spikes as the sound of pointed heels on the concrete draw my attention from my insecurities to a wildly tall, wildly beautiful woman that walks confidently along the line. Her hair is a shocking fall of silver-gray, her skin a lovely, smooth shade of black that is a startling contrast to the faded gray-green shade of her eyes. She's so beautiful, she doesn't even feel human to me. She looks like something other. Something mythical, which is what I'm guessing she's going for.

"Persephone!" a female voice calls from across the street, snapping my attention from the woman with the silver-gray hair to my supervisor. Beth is in her early thirties, but she's been talking about going out all week long. She just broke up with her boyfriend, and she's on the hunt for a good time.

She's also determined to call me by my birth name, even though I've told her repeatedly to call me Annie. That's the trouble with formal documents. People have access to your real name, and if they choose, they can use it. Beth thinks my name is too cool, considering what we do and the site we're working on excavating, to *not* call me by my given name.

Luckily, the rest of the team calls me Annie.

I'm waving to Beth when the woman moves in front of me, cutting my view of Beth. Her unique eyes slide over me from tip to toe, and back again, before her perfect lips part. She says something I don't understand, before following it with, "Persephone?"

I blink up at her. She emanates a kind of power I have no experience with. Her white suit is fitted to showcase the round curves and sharp lines of her lithe body. The plunge of her suit jacket is alarmingly low, and I can't help but feel my cheeks flare with heat as I tip my head to meet her striking eyes.

"I—I don't u-understand," I stutter, hating that I sound so immature in *her* presence. So caught up by her beauty.

Her head tips to the side only slightly, eyes studying my face as though she's attempting to see through me. Then, perfectly spoken English sounds between us. "Your name is Persephone?"

I nod. "Um. Yeah, it is."

I don't think she has a Greek accent at all.

Her eyes search mine, flaring with something that strikes a chord of alarm deep within me. "These are your friends?"

"Yes," I say as Beth arrives with her girlfriend in tow.

Gray-green sweeps over the women and she oddly says, "All such beautiful flowers."

Claire giggles and Willa makes a noise between a laugh and incredulous offense, but, thankfully, she says nothing.

Silver, as I'm coming to call the woman, waves her hand toward the entrance. "You are all exquisite." Her eyes never leave mine. "Please, take the VIP line inside." She pulls a black card embellished with gold from her jacket pocket, handing it to me with silver-painted nails. "Tell the man at the door that Leuce sent you."

My heart jolts, my love of myth colliding with my understanding of reality as I gape at her. "Your name is Leuce? Like the nymph?"

"You are knowledgeable of Greek mythology?" she asks curiously, one silver brow cocked in interest. "Specifically, the mythology of Hades?"

"I—I love Greek mythology." *Why do I feel like I could stand here and talk to this woman all night?* She intimidates me, and yet, there is a piece of her that feels somehow, bizarrely, known to me.

I'm losing the plot. Really, I am.

She smiles. Behind me, someone gasps. Her effect clearly extends to more than just me, and for that, I'm grateful. At least I'm not the only one ensnared by her unique beauty.

"Is it really so shocking that my name be Leuce when yours is Persephone?"

"It's just—um—it's quite a coincidence, is all."

She gives me that delicate head dip again. "How so?"

"My name is Persephone. I'm visiting a club owned by a man whose name is allegedly Hades, and I'm meeting a woman who works for him named Leuce. Just a little bizarre, I guess."

She smirks. "Wait until you meet Minthe."

"Oh, now that's just too much," Willa says, moving closer to me.

Leuce's smirk widens into a full-blown smile. Her unique eyes twinkle. "There is always the possibility that they're stage names, of course."

"That makes sense." Willa nods, sliding her arm through mine. "I bet everyone in this club has a mythical stage name."

I'm inclined to agree with her, because the alternative really is just too much. Still, I can't help but ask, "And Hades?"

Leuce's eyes flare bright. "What of Hades?"

Good God, the way she purrs his name. It's—I don't even know what it is.

"Is his name real?"

"I assure you, Persephone, that Hades is very, very real."

"I mean his name, not him. Of course, the God of the Underworld isn't real. I'm talking about the man who owns this club. The one they call Hades. Is that a stage name, too?"

"Like I said, Hades is very real, Persephone." She waves her hand to the now empty VIP line. "Please, go ahead and enjoy your time in the Tower of Pluto."

FOUR

ades

THE BLADE SLIDES into the scar across my palm, splitting it wide as blood drips in a river from the wound to mix with the ashy powder in the bowl, thickening it into a paste. Once smooth, I pour the mixture into the paint I'll splash against the blank canvas enchanted by Hecate.

Wiping my palm clean of blood, I tie my hair back, slide onto the stool, and lift my brush. I don't blink or breathe until I'm disturbed by a noise from behind. I realize I'm halfway through a painting, my thoughts far away as the colors mesh into a disturbed prison of charmed canvas and blood.

The sound of an ash rock spit from the depths of the river Phlegethon is dropped into a bowl fashioned from the skull of Uranus, my grandfather. I defeated him in a brutal and bloody battle that took place shortly after myself and my brothers had imprisoned our father, and the rest of the Titans. It had been a battle unlike any other the earth has seen, or hopefully, will ever see again.

It had been assumed Uranus had died after Cronus castrated him. Assumed, but never proven. He'd simply taken to the sky to lurk in wait, for his time to strike for the power he once knew. A power I was unwilling to lose, being the young and ambitious God I was when I first claimed the throne of the dead.

His return had been the mark of his physical end as I drained him of blood, stripping his soul of flesh and bone. It is his blood that bubbles and boils in the river Phlegethon, his furious rage that sears the souls held captive within Tartarus, ringed by the inescapable river Phlegethon.

I understand his ire. The world in which he created, the lives he crafted to worship him, had slain him. I understand that Uranus is a dangerous and powerful thing that must be kept contained. I understand that such a thing is within the scope of my responsibility as God of the Underworld, and keeper of evil. I have shouldered this burden with the utmost seriousness for millennia.

But I am tired. I am angry and I am resentful.

I am vengeful.

That which has always been my motivation, my utmost treasure, was schemed from me in a terrible, unforgivable play of betrayal.

For her, for my love, *my wife*, I have never stopped searching.

If it weren't for the Fates vowing that she would be reborn, I'd have loosed Uranus' immortal soul, and all the Titans in a damning play for revenge. I would have cast the venom of my grief wide on this Earth, destroying all that they cherish. All who worship them. I would have locked the gates of the Underworld, closing my realm from the chaos I released, damning them all above. Protecting only the souls I've vowed to keep safe within my realm.

But the curse of my past has been intricately woven into the fabric of the future, and I am trapped in the prison of my grief. I am bound by the shackles of my hatred for the spite of a mother. *My sister.* Demeter.

The bitch.

The ash rock grinds into the unbreakable skull of Uranus, disintegrating to dust under the smooth bone I pulled from his forearm. His bones are the strongest element on earth. A thousand times stronger, even, then Tungsten, the current, and wrongly suspected strongest element in the world.

If they knew how valuable, how undefeatable, the bone of a Titan was, governments would thrust armies at me in bid to infiltrate Tartarus. Little do they or the other Olympians know, that the Titans are no longer held prisoner within Tartarus. They are bound to a prison world that is entirely their own, and of my crafting.

I am the singular keeper. The beast holding the key to their damnation. I have fed them, nourishing their hatred. Their lust for vengeance.

I will continue to keep them, to pour my blood and strength into their prisons—until I have found her.

I inhale deep into my lungs, tasting the familiar, sweet scent of mint. With a roll of my shoulders, I dip the brush into a pool of murky blue. For a moment, the painting comes alive. A scream of tortured rage slithers from the canvas, swept up and sealed away in another brushstroke.

Minthe's seductive voice crawls in the space between us. "Who was that?"

"Oceanus."

"Ah," she sings. "The blue. You're giving him an ocean this time?"

"I think it's fair." I wipe my hands of the paint. "He suffered for the last century in a desert. He's parched."

"Of course, he is." Minthe smiles, a wicked and lovely thing. It falters as she scoops the ground dust into a jar that she seals with a lid. She turns to face me and I wait, knowing what is coming before it dares to leave her lips. "What are you doing, Hades?"

"We've discussed this, Minthe."

"No, you've told me what you *won't* tell me. Why aren't they in Tartarus? Why haven't you told the Olympians?"

I feel the fire flash in my gaze, and watch as Minthe cringes. But only slightly. She's been with me too long to truly fear me.

I move away from my latest prison. The painting in which Oceanus will spend his foreseeable future, though I've had to rehome the Titans far sooner than I'd like, the binds of my prisons weakening like the rest of me. I settle behind the sprawling desk I've had crafted from the same obsidian that veins the white stone of this tower.

I pin Minthe with eyes the color of coal. "Hang the painting when it is dry."

Her mouth tightens. I raise a brow when it parts, because I think she's about to give me attitude. *That just won't do.*

She is saved when my attention cuts to the swinging door of my office. My teeth grind behind my scowl. "Has everyone forgotten who I am tonight?"

Leuce, braver even than Minthe, struts into my space. She heads straight for Minthe, gripping her around the neck and pulling her in for a deep, penetrating kiss.

I feel no arousal as I watch. I very rarely feel anything at all anymore.

Aside from anguish and rage, that is.

My pitifully eternal soul weeps. The echo of my grief screaming her name within the endless depths of me.

Leuce breaks the kiss and turns to me with a wide, cat-like smile. Her gray-green eyes, the color of a white poplar's leaves bleached by heat, flash as they meet mine.

I feel an unusual flutter in my chest.

A quickening of hope.

She strolls casually across the room, her heels clicking with the heavy beat of my pulse before she settles her palms on my desk, silver nails sharp against the obsidian slab. She leans close, her voice like dripping honey.

She tells me, "I found her."

FIVE

P*ersephone*

MY EARS ARE STILL RINGING from the last scream of my name in his familiar voice. Never, not ever in my life has it ever sounded so loud as it did only minutes ago. The grief. The rage-infused anguish. It's so close I feel I might reach out and touch it. *Him.* I fear I might walk into it with every step I take as I put distance between me and the girls.

My vision bursts between sharp and blurred images as I move, disoriented and panicked. Maybe I really am losing my mind. Maybe I do have something deeply, inherently wrong with me. I'm hearing voices. No, not voices. A single, specific voice. But does it matter how many there are when it's a constant in my mind?

With a shaking hand, I reach out to steady myself against the wall. I've found myself in a big, hexagonal shaped, windowless room. There is only a single arched entrance from which I came. I'm not sure how I ended up here. If it was a hall I took or stairs.

I'd been fleeing, I realize. Fleeing that which I have no hope of escaping. My own mind is a treacherous place. A prison I was born to, and I fear it's a prison I'll die within.

People chatter as they roam the room, pausing to consider the art that has been hung on the walls. My skin feels dewy, either from the escape I attempted to make or the nerves that thrash inside with the quick violence of a whip.

My knees wobble as my gaze shifts from the people in the room, to the painting closest to me. Something about it has my pulse quickening. It pulls me closer, as though the talons in the painting have stretched from the canvas to claw at the threads of my ravaged soul, tugging me nearer. It's a gory piece, there's no denying it.

It's not the style that usually grips me, for I am typically drawn to the heartsore pain of a lost love. A tragic end to a beauty that never got the chance to *be*. My heart is a glutton for the worst kind of punishment within the strokes that caress a canvas. Always seeking the romance that never blooms. The love that never flies. The passion that, tragically, dies.

This painting is not that. It is raw, however. Upon a more intimate inspection, I see that it's not just talons that reach out from the painting, as though to snare the viewer. But it's the leafless limbs of a starved tree, billowing in a violent wind. Behind the curled talons is a thing of darkness. It is faceless, boneless, and yet, somehow, humanoid. Beyond the disembodied darkness, torn pieces of flesh and shattered bone burst outward to shimmer in the vastness of a deep ebony streaked with depthless blue, that I realize in horror, depicts an endless night of suffering. The stars are the flesh and bone that have been torn from —what? A dark soul? And holding it all together, imprisoning a galaxy of torment, is the taloned tree that roots to nothing, swimming in a lifeless, endless eternity.

It's tragic. Utterly, completely, *painfully tragic.*

"What do you think?"

I blink, startled by the deep warmth within the man's voice. It's like being enveloped by sin and flame and the kind of darkness that makes you want to close your eyes and settle in for a long, dreamless sleep.

What the hell, Annie?

"About what?" I ask disjointedly. I can't seem to tear my gaze from the painting to look at him. I'm held captive by the horror. A prisoner of paint.

"The painting." I think I hear amusement, and it's the thing that draws my gaze to him.

I'm struck. He's—well, he's—I—I'm speechless.

A hot blush climbs from the deep of my belly. An inferno of dormant hormones suddenly bursting like a pin-pricked balloon in the depths of me. It paints my too-pale skin a deep shade of pink. My mouth goes bone dry.

God, save me.

As though he heard my mental plea, the corner of his full mouth twitches. He tips his head ever so slightly toward the painting, prompting in his deep timbre, "The painting."

I blink. My mind is blank. I parrot weakly, "Th-the painting?"

The twitch of his lips tugs into a half grin. The knock I feel against my heart is physical. "What do you think of the painting?"

"Ohhh." I cover my burning cheeks with cool hands. I can't even blame my obliviousness on having a drink, because I didn't have a single one.

The man slides his big hands into the pockets of his fitted suit as he waits. I can't help but give him a quick once-over before I force my gaze back to the painting. He's *that* handsome. And that's saying something, considering I can't recall ever having a crush on anyone. In fact, I'd been so unmoved by attraction, for either girl or boy, that I thought I might be asexual.

If I'm taking into consideration the tingling heat I feel between my legs right now, I'm going to say I'm not asexual at all. Apparently, all I needed to get me going was a man twice my age. Okay, maybe I'm being just a tad dramatic, but the guy has to be touching thirty-five. Maybe even thirty-seven.

I can't believe I'm entertaining these thoughts.

Things are wrong with me. Big things. Dad would lose his mind if he knew I was getting all tingly for a man in his thirties.

I do my best to banish the tingles as I consider the painting again. What *do* I think of it?

I steal a breath that tastes oddly of woodsmoke, earth, and something else. Something unknown. Thoughts of epic tragedy fill my mind, but instead of forming an eloquent reply, I blurt, "I think the artist is crazy." There's a deep chuckle beside me, but I hurry to explain, "I mean, I'm not the best judge of sanity. I'm pretty sure I'm mad, too."

What in the heck is wrong with me? Shut up, Annie. Shut. Up!

"And, might I ask, what has your sanity in question?"

I can literally *feel* myself attempt to swallow the words, but when I open my mouth, they tumble out in a blast of truth that has the blood draining from my face in one quick whoosh. "I hear a voice in my head."

I'll never recover from this.

He arches a single brow. I decide I've already blown apart whatever interest called him over to me in the first place. I may as well continue trudging full speed down the damning tracks of truth.

This train has left the station, and there's no going back.

Grammy always said there's no point in being embarrassed about what has already transpired. You can't change the past, and as long as you're moving forward, you're going in the right direction.

I forge ahead, lifting a single finger between us. "Just one voice. I'm not a complete lunatic. I've heard him since I was little." His eyes drift over my face when I scrunch my nose. Quietly, I admit, "I can't recall a time when I didn't hear him."

"What does he say to you?"

"Nothing. He doesn't ever say anything *to* me."

His head tips, and there is curiosity in his dark eyes. "Then what do you hear?"

"He calls my name. That's it."

His eyes are so impossibly dark as they search mine. When his lips part, I wet my own. His eyes drop to chase the movement, flickering with something that snares the breath in my chest. It looks an awful lot like hunger. A ravenous, starved, dangerous hunger.

I excuse it away with innocent ignorance. I'm not experienced enough to know what hunger looks like. Much less hunger on a man like him.

"What *is* your name?" Am I wrong, or has his voice

dropped in pitch? And why does it suddenly ring with the familiar undercurrents of the voice I've only ever heard in my head?

My name falls between us on a breathless breath. "Persephone."

CHAPTER
SIX

*ades*

THE URGE TO lift her into my arms and steal her away to the Underworld is strong. So strong, I have to shove my hands into my pockets. Such an act did not bode well for me the first time. I suspect that tossing this lovely creature, my wife reborn, over my shoulder and carrying her away to a world she knows only as damnation, would go over even less successfully now. In this new time where people walk the earth unaware of the Gods that continue to rule above, around, and, well, under them.

When did we stop demanding reverence from the

pitiful people born in our image? How was it we allowed the birth of new gods and their religions to amass the following they possess today, essentially wiping away our memory and labeling it myth?

Even now, Olympus grows restless. Inside the seas, Poseidon rages. His rage has washed away entire cities, and yet they remain ignorant, praying to a God in the sky as they once prayed to my grandfather, Uranus, before Cronus plucked him from the sky to cut the flow of his seed and end his reign of misery. Before I stripped him of flesh and bone and cast him to the sky of a world within my own realm, a cage of my creation, a prison.

I imagine it now, though. Taking her for my own. Sinking inside her. Possessing her.

My blood heats like the fires of Tartarus, burning me from the inside as desire swirls. An unchecked storm of chaos and need threatening to devour me as I was once devoured by the insecurities of my father, freed only by the ego of my brother.

I can see myself taking her, claiming her, even now. In complete disregard for the way the people would watch, would scream their outrage at the injustice of her stripped freedom. As though they have a right to this freedom our laziness has allowed them to, falsely, believe they possess.

But no. I must pause. I must wait. I must do it differently this time.

This time I will not force her to take a stand at my

side. I will not force myself inside her body. I had been a young God when I'd allowed my obsession with her beauty to morph me into a being of desire, stripped of all rational control.

I am not young now. Now, I am ancient.

And the goal is not simply her body. It is the entirety of her heart, and the eternal life of her soul. For if I'd had her soul the first time, they never could have done what they'd done. Never could have stripped me of all that was her, casting me to live what felt like an eternity of torment without her.

No, now that I've found her, I will not rest until I possess all the parts of her. Until the soul I've loved for eternity is stitched to the very fabric that weaves mine, knotted in such a way that even the Fates cannot unravel the ties that bind us.

Her lips part, little tongue teasing out to wet full lips stained a lovely shade of rose pink. The urge to lean in and capture her mouth beneath mine, to taste her lips, is like a stab through the gut.

It's been too long.

She speaks. "I don't know why I told you my name is Persephone. No one calls me that."

"Is it not your name?" I already know it is, know it's her. There are slight physical differences, of course, to the young Goddess I'd claimed as my wife eons ago. But I've ached for her memory long enough to see that within this lovely body, under this creamy flesh, behind those emerald eyes, is the same soul—the *only* soul I've ever truly loved.

She has finally, after too long, been reborn.

And just in time for the stirrings of an Olympic war.

I feel my jaw pulse, a rare physical allowance into the truth of my emotions. Her eyes widen in response, my perceptive little wife.

Of course, she doesn't know she's mine. But it won't be long.

As though sensing the building magnitude of my ageless obsession, she takes a quick step back from me. The urge to chase, to devour every ounce of space that dares take form between us, is so strong that standing still nearly takes me to my knees.

She lifts a delicate hand to push lovely waves of white-blonde hair behind an elven tipped ear. A feature she shares with Demeter even now, born of another.

Her voice is soft, and I imagine the way her sighs and cries will fall when I root myself deep within her. "It is my name. But, um—" She swallows. I make her nervous. *Why do I like that?* "Everyone calls me Annie."

"Annie?" I frown. Such a mortal name for a girl intended to be much, much more.

She nods. "Annie."

"I like Persephone."

She snorts, and I feel my head notch back on my

shoulders. When I arch a brow, she rewards me with a small laugh. *Music.* "You would be the only one."

That can't be true. "Tell me, Persephone, where are you from?"

"Canada. Alberta."

The land of wheat. It shouldn't surprise me, that Demeter would plant her daughter's soul in such a place. Her ego is no more checked now than it had been long ago.

"And your parents?" Even as I ask, I already know. Already suspect.

Her smile is soft, and there is gentle love in the fresh youth of her expression. "Dad's a farmer. Mom owns a flower shop in town."

Of course, she does. Of course, he is. "What crop does he produce?"

"Wheat, mostly."

Fucking Demeter. "And what brings you to Greece?"

I watch as her head tips slightly to the side, and she studies me. I think, curiously, that she's contemplating truth or lie. *She is riveting.*

She wets her lovely lips again, and inside my pants, my cock stirs. She's can't know it, but she's driving me mad.

My willpower is nearing its limits.

Finally, she admits reluctantly, "The voice, I think."

Is it possible that this voice she hears is mine? The desperate call of a soul tethered by a single, frayed string, to hers?

"How so?" Even I can hear the eagerness in my question for her reply.

"Well..." She pauses to consider. "I've always felt drawn to the myths of Greece."

People today and their myths. I encourage, "Go on."

She pulls in breath. "In grade six, we had a unit on Ancient Greece. It was the spark of a lifelong love for all things Greek Mythology. I studied in my own time, and somehow felt closer to the call I heard in my mind. Initially, that voice only ever sounded when I was in sleep. It would wake me," she admits. "I told my parents and they took me to doctors who toyed with the idea, I might be mentally unstable. Plagued with a personality disorder, early onset bipolar, potential schizophrenia..." She waves her hand, and a flush of pink stains her cheeks. "I started to understand how dangerous that might be for me, and told them it stopped. I've hid the fact I hear this unnamed man calling my name from everyone since. You're the first—"

She laughs to herself in disbelief. "You're the first person I've told. Anyway, more recently, I began hearing him outside of sleep. Maybe it's the fact I felt closer to his call when I studied the ancient myths, but I developed an interest for art and archaeology. I can't paint to save my soul, but I can dig." She pulls in a big breath, her breasts rising under the thin white dress my fingers itch to tear from her flesh. "I'm here on a

41

summer archeology program now. If I like it, I'll peruse a further education."

"Do you like it?"

She smiles a bright and beautiful smile that nearly slays me. She's beautiful. So beautiful. I haven't seen a beauty such as hers in so, so achingly long.

"I love it."

"No desire to follow in the steps of your parents?"

Her face softens again. It is clear she loves them dearly. I can't help but wonder, how strong the bonds she feels to these people who have been given the soul of my wife to care for.

From what I've already heard, I am uncertain if I find them worthy.

"I love gardening. Mom says I have a natural affinity for plants. It seems that, with a single touch, I can bring life into a dying plant. I know, instinctively, what they need, whether it be sunlight or water or someone to talk to." She blushes again, her eyes dipping down before she peers up through thick, golden lashes at me. "Did you know plants flourish under conversation? Under connection?" She doesn't wait for me to answer. "I love plants, tending and caring for them. Watching them grow. But to answer your question..." She shrugs. "I guess I want more from life than what Mom and Dad have. Something different."

Nothing she said surprises me. After all, she is Demeter's daughter. The immortal soul in her body is that of my wife, Goddess of spring and fertility and love.

She is the seed of nourishment to all life, once worshiped by God and man alike. I, however, never stopped worshipping her.

"Annie! Oh my god, girl, I've been looking everywhere for you!" A girl Persephone's age with dark skin and sleek hair hurries toward us. "You ran off like hellhounds chased you. What happened?"

I scowl. Cerberus would never chase her. Well, maybe to lick, but...

Persephone's skin tints with a pretty blush. She shifts nervously. "I just—I needed a moment. There was a lot of people and I—well, I really came for the art."

"Of course, you did." The girl rolls her eyes as she loops her arm through Persephone's, tugging her back in her unconscious quest to put space between us. This is something I am used to. People, from the beginning of time, have given me a wide berth. They sense, not unfairly, that I am a dangerous being they should be wary of. But with her—with Persephone—after all this time longing for her, searching for her, *aching* for her—watching someone attempt to pull her away from me has something sharp snapping inside me.

I move swiftly, blocking the single exit. Her friend looks at me like the predator I am, and have always been to this inferior species.

The girl narrows dark eyes on me, but Persephone's emerald eyes widen. They are filled with such sweet, alarmed innocence. It reminds me of the way she'd once looked at me. That first time as I appeared in the garden where she played with her friends in the moments before I stole her away.

Irritatingly, it is the girl who speaks. "Who's this?"

"Willa, this is..." *I haven't told her my name.*

I extend my hand to Persephone, folding her small one in mine as I introduce, "Hades."

The shock of electricity as I touch her for the first time rivals the bolts Zeus throws around. Her bright emerald eyes widen in a moment of alarmed shock that is interrupted by her friend, Willa.

"Hades? Hades as in Hades Pluton? The owner of this club?" Without releasing Persephone's hand, I nod. Willa throws her arm wide to indicate the art on the walls. "Artist of all *this*?"

I reply, my voice darkly low. "One and the same."

Persephone looks truly horrified. "I—I called you crazy."

I smirk. "You called yourself crazy, as well. I take no offense."

"Oh, my God." An embarrassed flush taints her pale skin. I want to taste every inch of it, soaking the burn of her emotion into myself through my lips on her skin. "I'm so sorry."

"You called him crazy?" Willa interrupts, and Persephone tears her eyes from mine.

I have to swallow the dark violence that bubbles inside me. *I want her gaze on me, only me.*

I am an obsessive God.

"I'm—I'm so sorry." Her eyes flicker to mine and away again. "We should go."

No.

"Right." Willa nods. I feel something deadly building inside me. The restraint I cling to shatters, the desperate need to abduct her to the Underworld—to the safety of my domain—rages under the calm control of my surface.

The fear I feel that I might lose her before I really have her is colossal.

Willa speaks again. "Gotta get you home so you can look for that job tomorrow."

Electricity hums over the surface of my skin, stirring the ancient God that hovers under the surface of my flesh. *He is ready to slay all that comes between us.* "You're looking for a job?"

Persephone nods again. "I spent most of my savings on the program and flights. I—I need a job if I'm going to survive the stay."

"How convenient." I flash her a grin that has her eyes falling to my mouth. I wonder if she feels this connection the way I do, despite the brutal attempts Demeter fell to in order to make her forget. "I'm looking to hire."

Her brows rise, big green eyes widening. "You want me to work for you?"

"Why not?"

"Um—" She glances around us before she sucks in a shuddering breath. "I don't know that I'm suited to this work."

"What work is that, specifically?" I need to know what it is she won't do, so that I might offer her something she will do. *Anything to keep her.*

"Working in a club." She cringes. "This isn't my scene. Like I said, I came for the art."

I want to tell her that I have more art. Hundreds of unseen paintings. I want to lure her away from this friend—from her life. I force what I hope is an easy smile as I slip the hands that itch to steal her away into my pockets. "Well, lucky for me, I'm not looking for someone for the club."

She releases the lip she's been biting. "You're not?"

My blood is a typhoon whirling inside my body. "No."

"What are you looking for?"

Whatever keeps you as close to me as possible. I say smoothly, "A personal assistant."

CHAPTER

SEVEN

P *ersephone*

THE UNIVERSE clearly has a sense of humor, and I'm the obvious butt of the joke.

I don't know what possessed me to agree to meet the man for an interview to a job I have no business entertaining taking. My work experience includes growing plants, arranging bouquets, and punching orders into a tablet connected to a register. Oh, and if pressed, I can bump along in a tractor.

It absolutely does not include the experience one would need to work as the personal assistant to a man such as Hades Pluton. A man who inherited millions and transformed it to billions. A complex man who mostly keeps to himself. Rumored to be tortured, arrogant, distantly cold, and sometimes cruel. Not unlike the God of ancient myth, his namesake.

Of course, I'd *Googled* him deep into the night while Willa snored in the bed next to mine.

Now, I'm sleep-deprived on my day off from digging this week, and I'm about to sit for an interview with a man named Hades. Hence being the butt of a universal joke. *Because what are the odds?*

The walk from the house I'm currently staying in with some of the other students of the program, to the Tower of Pluto takes longer than I'd like. For the first time since meeting her, I wish I was Claire. With her private apartment in the city and car paid for by wealthy and supportive parents to get her where she needs to be, her life in comparison to mine feels pretty cushy. If I had my own place—or at the very least, my own room, I might get a full night's sleep.

Really, as much as I like Willa, it would be nice if I didn't have to listen to her snore. Also, if I get this job, it would be nice to live a little closer to the Tower.

We'd taken a taxi the night before, and it's not like I haven't walked by the club before in my explorations. But walking in this heat while panicking isn't fun, even though I'd thought I could use the exercise to burn off a layer of nerves.

All I've really done is sweat through my clothes.

This is a waste of time. The man is *not* going to hire me.

I really don't know what I'm thinking. Hell, what had *he* been thinking, offering me the interview?

I'd told him I was insane. That I heard a voice in my mind and followed it to another country, for goodness' sake. And he thought, hey, let's hire the wack job to manage my personal affairs. *Honestly!*

Maybe he's the crazy one. The loopy-loo. One straw short of total insanity.

I mean, he'd have to be to hire a self-confessed crazy girl, right?

As instructed, I enter through the main doors of the Tower, where a gigantic man with bulging muscles peeking out from short sleeves gives me a curious once-over. He's sitting at a table close to the door, and I get the sense his purpose there had been to wait for me.

That sense is confirmed when he rises from his seat to lumber to the door, flipping a heavy bolt. He turns to me. "Persephone?"

I point to the door. "I think you should have asked me that *before* you locked me inside."

He smirks, a wide and confident grin. "Hades is waiting for you. Leuce will take you to him." He gestures behind me, and only then do I hear the clicking of heels on marble.

I turn to find the woman from outside the club walking toward me. Again, she's in a bright white outfit. But unlike last night, she's showing more skin today in a white pantsuit and a sheer white camisole.

Again, I'm hit by her beauty. Next to her, sweaty like I am, I feel notably inferior.

"It's good to see you again, Persephone," Leuce greets me in her smooth voice.

"You too. And, please, call me Annie."

Leuce gives me a curious smile and an even more curious shake of her head. I can't tell if she's laughing at me or refusing to call me by my preferred name.

"This way." With a hand on the small of my back, she guides me from the entrance toward a wall I hadn't noticed the night before. It opens into an elevator. I step inside with her before shimmying out from under her touch.

She clearly notices, and I am left explaining shyly, "It's hot out, and I walked from my apartment." I cringe. "I'm sweaty."

Leuce straightens her shoulders, and the result has her braless breasts pushing against her translucent shirt. I'm shocked as I catch a glimpse of dark nipples, and force my burning gaze to the cool floor.

I think she is amused, as a low and breathy sound falls from perfectly painted lips. "Sweat is normal, Persephone. As is admiring a beautiful body."

Heaven help me. I'm so hot, I think I might melt.

I'm shaking with nerves. Clearly, I don't know what to do with this confident woman.

"You can look," she tells me gently. "I will like it."

I do look at her, meeting her bold gaze. The overwhelming confidence has envy spiking like a spear inside me. What I would give to be so sure within the skin I wear.

She pushes away from the wall to close the distance between us. As she towers over me, I swear I catch the scent of a crisp mountain breeze. Hear the rustle of leaves on the wind.

With a small shake of my head, I refocus on her face. Watching her as she studies me. She murmurs, "You are going to change everything."

I have no idea what she means, and am unable to ask as the doors roll open into a private lobby. My steps stutter as she enters the very clearly private space with the same confidence she owns in every move she makes. Noticing that I don't follow, she pauses to spin on one dagger-like silver heel.

"Come, Persephone. Hades waits."

Swallowing my nerves, I do as she requests. I follow her into what kind of feels, terrifyingly, like my own damnation.

HADES SITS in front of an easel, perched on a black stool with both feet flat on the floor. There's a tension in the way that he moves, the brush sweeping blood red paint across a canvas colored in deeper, countless shades of red. The painting isn't near complete, and yet I get the terrifying sense that the very canvas is oozing blood.

His long, loose waves are pulled into a bun at the back of his head, but more than a couple strands have fallen loose. Although he's wearing black suit pants, he's shucked his shirt to display a ripple of muscle stacked on muscle.

I got the sense the man was massive the night before, but I hadn't expected him to be *this* big.

Really, if the man so wished, I'm confident he could crush me like a bug.

"Hades," Leuce calls after a moment, startling me.

I don't know how I'd forgotten her presence, but I feel my face turn pink with the realization that she definitely caught me checking out her boss. My potential boss.

Frick, frick, frick.

This day just keeps getting worse. I'm clearly sleep deprived.

Hades' entire form stiffens. His shoulders and back expand in a way that makes me think he's inhaled a big breath, before he places the brush into a holder and slides smoothly from the stool. For a man so large, he moves with a kind of lethal grace that feels just a little unnerving.

His eyes find and lock on me, never shifting as he dismisses in his deep voice, "Thank you, Leuce."

Leuce gives him a small nod, flashing me a knowing smile. I wish I knew what she knew, I think, as she turns on her spiked heels and exits. The door clicks closed behind her, leaving me entirely alone with Hades. I can't help my flinch.

He lifts a rag, wiping at the paint that clings to his skin as he takes a step closer. Nerves shoot through my body, spraying buckshot into every corner of me. My body trembles.

One of two things happen when I'm extremely nervous or extremely uncomfortable. I babble or I shut down.

Today, as it would have it, I babble. A lot. "Don't you think this is a little odd?" I don't wait for him to reply before my tongue is wagging again. "I'm Persephone and you're Hades." I laugh nervously. "That's just—it's—well, what are the odds?" Again, I give no pause. "I mean, of course, I know we're not *the* Persephone and Hades, because that would just be ludicrous. I'm insane, but not *that* insane." *Oh, God, I'm so not getting this job.* "I mean, I obviously know that we're not them. We aren't going to—"

I snap my mouth closed when he comes close enough to smell before he stops moving. His dark eyes are fixed on me, and only me. It's like he's drinking me in, devouring me without even touching me. Trepidation runs a cool finger over my soul. I swear to all that is holy, I feel a pull in a place so deep inside of me, as though the very core of my being is threaded to this man, and he's just given it a single firm tug.

He dips his head only slightly, his hands still

twisting in the rag between us. "What is it we're not going to do, Persephone?"

Holy crap—I can't think when he's this close. Forming words is a struggle, so I don't think about what I say before I say it. "Fall in love. Escape to the Underworld together."

I'm blowing this interview.

"Is that what they did?"

I blink. "What?"

"Did Hades and Persephone *escape* together into the Underworld?"

"I don't know." His eyes lift from mine to the frown between my brows. "I—he—he abducted her."

"He did." His voice is a low, rough purr. "He saw her in a field of flowers, playing with her little friends."

"She was a child."

"Not quite a child. Not entirely a woman," he corrects. I shiver under the sweep of intense eyes. "Times were different."

Something about his final statement has a laugh bubbling between us. I slap my hand over my mouth to sever the sound before saying with confidence, "It's myth. None of it ever happened."

He's not dissuaded. "Do you think she loved him?"

"I don't know. Can a woman love a man who abducts her from all that she knows?" I'm lying. I've been obsessed with the love between Hades and Persephone since I learned of their existence. But I don't want him to know that. Not yet.

He's so still, I'm not even sure he's breathing. "Do you think he loved her?"

I shrug. It's a small lift and fall of my shoulders, but his eyes catch the movement. I think he catches all my movements, every breath, every flutter of my pulse. No one has ever looked at me the way he looks at me.

Or maybe my infatuation with my potential boss, who happens to be way too old for me, is putting hopeful things into my mind. Things that don't exist.

I need to put an end to this. So, squaring my shoulders, I say, "I don't think they were real. I think ancient people were desperate to make sense of things, of their life and their death, and they created elaborate stories to explain away these unexplainable things. There is no Underworld or Hades. There is no Persephone or pomegranate or abduction or love. There is only myth."

Hades wets his lips, tosses his rag now streaked with blood red paint to the table next to his easel, and moves to put space between us.

I should be relieved, but I'm not. The space feels somehow wrong. Gaping.

With the heat that clings to him now gone, I'm enveloped in a bone-deep cold. Hugging myself, I wait for him to speak again, watching, as he lifts the black dress shirt from an obsidian topped desk. He dons it slowly, long, thick fingers working deftly at the buttons until he's appropriately dressed for an interview with a potential employee.

As for my part, I feel entirely undressed and stripped raw.

No man has ever affected me quite like Hades affects me. Maybe it's the dark romance of our ancient names, and the myth of the couple before us. The legend of their love. Maybe I really do have a thing for older men, and I'm only just now realizing it. Whatever it is, I endeavor to find a way to cut the head off this snake of infatuation before I am bitten and consumed by the venom of it.

I lift my chin. "I want to thank you for this opportunity, Hades, but I don't think I am suited to this job." *Whatever the job is.*

His black eyes lift to pin me in place. I couldn't move even if I wanted to. And sadly, I don't particularly want to.

Even though I know I should.

Working for this man—spending time with him—it would be dangerous.

And yet, even though I sense deep inside I should flee him, I can't make myself do it.

"I disagree," he says softly, but there is an edge of warning to his tone that suggests I don't tempt him. *I want to tempt him.* "I think you are exactly the thing that I need, Persephone."

EIGHT

P *ersephone*

"So, ESSENTIALLY, YOU WANT A MAID?" I'm dumbstruck. When I came here, I never imagined the job he would offer me would be *this*.

"No. I have a maid, Persephone." There is a shimmer in his eyes, a cock of his lips that suggests there's a joke in what he says next. "What I need is a wife."

"A w—" *He has to be joking.* I inhale a sharp breath through my nose and repeat more calmly, "A wife?"

"Without the legal documents." His eyes flicker with devious intention. He teases, "Unless you're interested, of course?"

My mouth falls open.

His lifts into a devilish smirk.

My eyes narrow and my hands find my hips. He seems to find this amusing, and it only serves to add a splash of gasoline to the fire he's set to burn inside me. I demand, "Are you playing with me?"

"I'm not known to play, Persephone."

"I don't understand." I shake my head dubiously. "You want me to do your laundry and pick up after you and coo—"

"As I said, I have a maid. She handles my laundry and the keeping of my private space."

Exasperation balloons inside my chest. I release it in a big breath. "Then what do you want from me?"

"As I said, I am aware that you have other obligations, what with your explorations into a career in archaeology. I can and will accommodate your prior commitments. What I need from you, what I am asking of you, is your time."

"My time?"

"As I explained, I would like you to come here after your days spent—digging. You said you can cook." I nod when he waits for confirmation. "I would like you to cook for me."

I don't understand why my heart is bludgeoning the cage of my chest. It's a simple conversation. A prospective position with a man any girl would be happy with.

"Every night?"

"Preferably. Unless you're demanding a night off."

I laugh, *because this man.* "Everyone needs a night off."

I swear his dark eyes twinkle. "Then we'll order in on your night off."

I'm speechless for an entire minute before I say exasperatedly, "I'll need a night off from you, Hades. To be alone. To explore the city. To hang out with friends. This is, technically, my second job, remember?"

His grin is slow. "Of course."

"So, that's all you want? Someone to cook for you?" *Why doesn't the man have a chef?*

"No. I want you to share the meals with me. I want you to spend time with me in the evenings, listen to me talk and talk in return. I want conversation and connection. And, occasionally, I would require you to accompany me to events I am unable to avoid, as my date."

"But we won't be dating. I won't sleep with you for money, Hades."

"I would never pay you to sleep with me, Persephone. I can assure you that sex is not something I am hard done by."

Not sex, I think sadly, a little stung for reasons I can't explain. Just human connection.

The man is, essentially, paying me to be his friend. His companion. Someone trustworthy enough to bring into his life as he might a wife, without the wifely benefits, of course.

It's devastating, really, if you think about it. He's so obviously wealthy, possessing so *much*, that he can't even trust the validity of a relationship. He's so extremely wealthy, so guarded and obviously used by those around him, that rather than sift through those truly and honestly available to him, he's hiring a fabricated version of the thing he desires.

He is lonely, I realize. The man has everything, and yet he is emotionally starved.

"Okay, so you want me to come here every day after my studies to cook, share dinner with you, tidy up and leave?"

His eyes bore into mine, and for a moment, I stop breathing. "I would like it if you were live-in."

"Live in?" I parrot dumbly. *This just keeps getting weirder, like I've stepped into the Twilight Zone.*

His lips twitch. "I like breakfast, too."

"You like—" I pause, inhale, and ask calmly, "Hades, it sounds like you need a cook."

He laughs. The sound is rich and unexpected and decadent. It touches me so deep inside, like a match to the marrow of my bones.

I'm struck breathless, immovable.

"You will share breakfast with me. I would like for it to feel natural between us. Friendly."

And we circle back to that. His need for companionship that is so out of touch for him, he's sought someone to hire to fulfill that need. A basic need no one should ever have to pay for.

I feel like a con artist for considering agreeing to this.

"Why me, Hades?"

He considers for a moment while I hold my breath in my lungs. "You are real and honest. Within minutes of meeting you, you admitted to me that you are crazy."

The breath bursts from my lungs on an abrupt laugh. "You want me as your companion because I told you I was a lunatic?"

"As I said, you're honest."

I shake my head, stupefied. "Hades, this is insane."

"What do you need to feel comfortable with this arrangement?" He stands from behind his desk, stalking closer to me until there are only inches between us. The scent of him, woodsmoke and sin and earth and something foreign surrounds me, scattering rational thoughts.

"I want to keep my room at the house, in case anything goes wrong."

"Done."

"I am supposed to get Saturdays and Sundays off. This week was funny with the schedule," I explain my odd days off. "It was the first week, and a little wacky. But I want at least one of those days to myself." He nods agreeably. "And this is a strictly professional arrangement, Hades. I'm serious when I said I won't sleep with you."

He assures, "I will have a room made up for you that is all your own."

I nibble my lips, feeling more than a little nervous and a lot uncertain. "Okay. I guess—I guess I'm working for you."

He smiles like a devil that just struck a deal for my soul.

I'm not altogether certain he didn't.

NINE

P *ersephone*

"LET ME GET THIS STRAIGHT." Willa drops another cube of sugar into her already sweet coffee. "You're moving in with the guy five days a week?"

"Essentially, yeah."

I don't bother correcting her and saying that I'd pretty much agreed to spend six days a week with a man I hardly know. In his house. As his...*companion*?

"Girl, that's nuts." She peers at me through furrowed brows, half her attention on the coffee she's stirring. "You just met him."

"I did."

"I think he's a psycho for even asking this of you."

I laugh, trying to put us both at ease. Inside, I've been a panicked mess since the totally bizarre interview/proposition I'd had with Hades yesterday. "You're the one who brought up I was looking for work. He just filled that need, I guess."

"Yeah, in a really creepy way."

"It's not creepy, Willa. It's sad."

Her head jerks back on her shoulders. "How is it sad? The guy's a billionaire. He can have anything he wants." She snorts. "He's as far from sad as sad can get."

"Just because he can afford a lot of things, doesn't mean he can get anything."

"Uh, that's exactly what it means. Look what he's doing to you."

"He's not *doing* anything to me." I'm starting to feel defensive, and that's making me feel annoyed. "He offered me a job, and I agreed."

"I just think he's taking advantage of you."

"He's not." At her disbelieving look, I say, "I don't need the money so much that he *can* take advantage of me. There are boundaries. I've made them clear, and he's agreed to respect them. If he suddenly opts not to respect my boundaries, there are plenty of other jobs. I'm sure I'd be able to get one."

"Then why don't you?"

"Why don't I what?"

"Get a different job."

I shrug. "I guess I'm curious."

She looks doubtful. "So, it has nothing to do with the fact the man is hotter than hades? Total pun intended."

"I'm not going there." But I can feel my face flaming. I shift in my own seat at the little table, thankful no one else has crawled out of bed yet, and try to attempt to conceal my discomfort with a sip of my coffee.

"Oh, come on. If you're taking this job with Mr. Rich and Steamy, you've got to at least give me the goods."

"There are no goods. There will be no goods." I huff. "I told you, it's strictly professional."

"Sure." She gives me big, disbelieving eyes and a hell of a snort. "Because that's going to last."

I hold firm. "It is. I would never sleep with my boss."

She gives me a look that says she doesn't believe me, and she can't wait to tell me she knew all along just how this was going to play out.

I sigh, feeling my shoulders fall. "I think he's just lonely, Willa. I think he has so much money that real relationships aren't something he trusts. Probably because most people think the way you do, and see him as nothing more than a bank sum."

Willa gasps in mock outraged affront. Then she rolls her eyes. "Okay, okay. I get it. You're a saint." She narrows her eyes at me. "What is he paying you?"

"I insisted on minimum wage."

"*Why* would you do that?"

I twist my lips to the side and admit, "It feels wrong that he would pay me more when he's really just paying for me to sleep, you know?"

"Okay." She takes a big gulp of her coffee. "I need a hot as hades man to pay me to sleep. Bonus points if his name is actually Hades. Hey, can I borrow yours?"

"Nope." I grin, but it is borderline forced. I know she's just playing with me, but the idea of sharing Hades in any capacity feels—wrong. Wrong in the kind of way that has nausea swirling in my belly and unease prickling my spine.

I don't like it. The very idea that I'm at all possessive of my boss has alarm bells ringing in my mind.

Willa pouts. "Seriously, it's not fair. How does this kind of thing even happen to people? And why am I never the people it happens to?"

I give her a smart little smile as I let my lips linger on the rim of my cup. "Probably because you see the negative first, and therefore miss your shot."

"I do not see the negative first."

"Was it not just you trying to talk me out of working for the creepy, but hot billionaire named Hades?"

"Whatever." She gives me an indignant sniff. "I still think you're crazy."

If only she knew just how on point she was.

"Maybe a little."

The sound of bare feet shuffling over tile has Willa

craning her neck as she peers to the side to see Theo lumbering into the little eat-in kitchen. With his eyes still half-closed in sleep, he doesn't see Addison come from the other side, and is unprepared for his attack. Having been together for the last week, both living and working close, things have gotten quite comfortable between most of us. We're like a little family, which is kind of a bad description if I'm being honest. Too many have either slept together, or have intentions of sleeping together, to be called family.

But since I have no intention of sleeping with anyone, I don't mind the little euphemism in my mind. It works for how I feel around them. How I'm coming to feel around them.

I'm entirely unsurprised when Addison reaches out to twist Theo's bare nipple. I'm even less surprised by the roar Theo lets out as his eyes snap wide and he shoots off after Addison for retribution. The two of them have gotten close fast, probably because they're nearly the same person.

Not only are they the same person, but they're both man-whores, said with the utmost respect, because although I don't engage personally in casual sex—or any sex, really, I know a lot of people like to.

The idea of casual sex blows my mind. No matter how I've tried, it's simply not something I understand. Maybe it's the way Mom and Dad have been together since high school. Maybe it's my upbringing in the church, although I've never felt particularly close to the God my parents' worship. Probably because, when I'd been a young child, afraid and hearing a voice in the deep of my mind, there had been no real comfort within the walls of my church. Where there should have been love, and acceptance, and healing, there had only been fear, and judgement, and divide. The sourness of my near damning diagnosis had clung to me in the years after, a stickiness I'd been unable to wash from my skin.

Maybe my lack of sexual interest has nothing to do with my parents or the church, after all. Maybe it has everything to do with the fact I've never felt the kind of attraction that would drive me to sexual exploration. At least not before now.

No, casual sex isn't something I engage in. But it's also not something I bother judging others for. How another wants to live their life is of no consequence to me.

Still, I can't help the realization, as I watch Addison catch Theo in a headlock, with his muscles and tan skin and floppy, golden blond curls, that maybe the sexual part of me I thought I lacked is finally awakening. Because I can't deny the tickle I feel in my belly as I watch the handsome boy all the girls giggle over and bat their lashes at, dominate—and wonder deep inside what it might be like to be the prey.

CHAPTER

TEN

ades

EVERYTHING IS SOFT AND, as both a hit to Demeter and a gift of comfort and familiarity to Persephone, floral. Soft neutrals accented in soft pink and softer green complement the warmth of sun gold and cloud white.

I'd decorated her room with the same magic I'd used and honed for centuries, gifted willingly by Persephone, at the wrath of Demeter, to craft not only the Elysium Fields, but the Isle of the Blessed, the Fields of Mourning, and the Asphodel Meadows, where an abundance of life thrives within the underworld.

Before I had crossed paths with the young girl who would become my wife—before she would become my Queen—my realms had been a dark and dank place, lacking life and meaning for the souls who met their living end to rest in my care.

I had been a creature of darkness, lacking patience or softness before her. I had ruled with a hand heavy of cruelty and demand, offering little in the way of *life* after death. I took what I desired with no care of consequence. In my domination of her soft body, my stealing of her tender heart, my determination to plant my seed of life within the girl destined to become the Goddess of spring, growth, and love, she taught me the ways of softness, of living. It was through her tears, her grief, and later, her gentle love, that I came to shed the shadows of darkness and violence to better my realms and myself. *For her.*

With her capture, the domination of her body and heart, seeds of life sprouted within the Underworld. The magic that flowed within her blood ran life into the rivers that fed the barren land. Her fertility stretched beyond her body to birth a paradise in what had been a realm of only darkness and despair, to become a place of life after death. A promise of something more.

It is for this reason Demeter had rained her wrath on us both. On the entire realm I ruled with her daughter, my Queen, at my side. She had tricked and schemed, lied, blackmailed, and maimed to see the destruction of our great love.

She had thought with the death of Persephone, the stealing of her eternal soul, that the new life in the Underworld would die. What she had not counted on was the gift of eternal life Persephone had bestowed upon me when she'd given me her love.

But life must always be fed, and without my Queen to give with her natural ease, my realm was left to feed upon the only thing it could. Me.

"How'd you manage this, Hades?" Minthe pulls a pastel green pillow veined with shimmering lines of a lighter green from the bed, giving it a gentle toss before she pulls it into her chest for a hug. Her sharp, slightly slanted green eyes are fixed on me, and as usual, her soil-colored bob, dagger straight, falls to frame her pixie-face.

Minthe, like Leuce, is beautiful. Exquisitely so.

I recall a time when I thought the two nymphs were the most beautiful women I'd ever seen. I'd been wrong.

"Yeah," Leuce agrees. "I'd like to know the same."

"I asked, and she said yes."

"It's not something you'd expect a girl her age to agree to," Leuce observes, sharp as a tack. "She's had two encounters with you and she's agreed to move in. At this rate, she'll be home in the Underworld within the week."

"That would be nice, Hades," Minthe says. "You won't be so weak anymore."

The mention of my ever-waning strength grates on my nerves like it always does. "It's not that simple."

"What isn't?" Leuce demands. "She clearly feels things for you."

"You know the curse of the Fates as well as I do." I spin to face the nymphs, barring Hecate and Charon, they are my oldest and most trusted friends. My family. "The consequences of Demeter's actions have made this more complicated than simply finding her again."

"Hades," Minthe says softly.

My rage erupts in a booming roar that sends a tremor through the Tower. "She was drowned in *The Lethe*."

Silence meets my eruption in a wash of grief that trembles the bones under my flesh. Leuce is the first to move, daring to close the space between us. She is smart enough, however, to refrain from touching me. "She will remember you. You will make her remember."

Minthe takes a hesitant step. "You will make her fall in love with you."

"She has no interest in love."

"Neither did she the first time." Leuce smirks, but there's sadness behind the act. "She won't be able to help it, Hades. The fall is unavoidable."

I had thought, with her return into my life, I would

find a stability the like I'd known before she'd been taken from me. An ease to rule that had been mine from the moment I helped capture the Titans.

I feel even less in control than I had in her absence. Because now, I know there will be forces at work that will try to pull her away from me. To steal her. And they will use any means at their disposal.

"Until I can take her to the Underworld, she will be in danger."

Minthe's face pinches in tight displeasure, but Leuce juts out her chin confidently. "We will protect her."

"She won't give up her archaeology program. If Demeter realizes she is here in Greece—" I can't finish. An image of her wrath flashes in my mind. Persephone, her beautiful, pale flesh bound by the black roots Demeter called from beneath the white sand bed of the river Lethe.

The heat of Tartarus moves unbidden through my veins, sweat prickling my flesh.

"I can join the program," Minthe's sweet voice offers, sounding through the buzz of eternal flames that crackle in my ears.

Leuce's head swivels to her mate. "That is an excellent idea. She hasn't met you. She won't suspect a thing."

Minthe's head bobs. "And I can protect her."

If there is one thing Minthe is accustomed to warding off, it is Demeter and her spiteful attacks.

I meet my friends' eyes, the fire cooling inside my blood. "I'll arrange it."

"I'll pack."

"Thank you, Minthe."

"It'll be my pleasure." Her smile trembles. "I miss her, too."

"I know."

ELEVEN

P *ersephone*

NOW THAT THE time has come for me to start *actually* working at Hades', I'm nervous. The entire taxi-ride here, I went over a thousand ways to tell him I can't do this. That I quit. If I had his number, I undoubtedly would have sent him my resignation through text, which is something I truly loathe about my generation. The cop out. The lack of face-to-face communication. The easy way. The ghosting.

It's all so immature, and probably a big reason I never found an attraction within my own age group.

All night last night, I tossed and turned under the spell of fiery dreams. Then, as I worked under the hot sun, I suffered the memories of my dreams that sent prickles of awareness over my flesh and set my blood to boil.

I truly hate the attraction I feel for the man who has become my boss. I hate that I want more from him than is appropriate. More than he could possibly want from me, considering the vast gap in our ages and experience.

Obviously, I'm no match for Hades Pluton. He's a man of experience and wealth. Our lives aren't compatible whatsoever.

Still, my silly dream-self spent the entirety of last night and half my waking day, concocting the fantasy of what it might feel like to have his full lips on my skin. To feel his hot breath snake down my spine, tugging shivers from the depths of me.

I need to get my head on straight or I'm going to mess this up royally.

The man wants a companion, not another phony after his dick and dough.

Eww. Just eww.

Scrubbing my hands down my face, I pay my fare and exit the taxi with my bag in hand. I enjoy cooking, but I don't have the slightest idea what I'm going to make tonight. I don't even know what Hades likes. I probably should have asked.

I'm so unprepared.

Swallowing another bloom of nerves, I shoot a smile and a soft, "Thanks," at the doorman who asks no questions as he lets me enter. My knees feel like Jell-O as I move straight for the elevator that will take me to Hades' apartment. He'd given me the private code to access his private space, which I punch into the panel with a trembling finger.

The climb in the elevator feels far too short. I feel dizzy and breathless with nerves as the doors roll open into his apartment. Feeling unsteady, I move into his space and flinch at the sound of the doors closing behind me.

God, what had I been thinking when I accepted this job?

"Hades?" I call, nerves spilling from me into the vast space that I now have a moment to take in. The floor and most of the furnishings are sleek black, lacking color. It's so unexpected, so barren when compared to the vibrant slash of color in his paintings, even if there is a sense of horror in the art he creates.

The walls are painted a color that reminds me of nature's violence. It's not quite gray, but not entirely purple. It's somewhere between, a cool glow, the color of the sun as it desperately attempts to penetrate a storm cloud. The light of the black iron chandelier, as it hangs from an impossibly high ceiling, casts an eerie and yet lovely glow onto the haunting color of his walls.

Clutching my bag, I kick off my shoes and move deeper into his space. The sprawling entrance opens into an extravagant kitchen and dining room done in polished black. Two steps down leads into a massive living room with a sectional big enough to host at least twenty people comfortably. I've never seen anything like the cushy black leather that sits on the plush black carpet before a massive black screen mounted to the purple-gray wall.

I'm not sure what it is about the couch that has my attention in a stranglehold. Maybe it's the fact it looks entirely unused, but clearly bought with the intention to entertain in some way, considering the size of it. The couch is a beast, not unlike the man who owns it.

I can't stop staring at the couch, wondering at the significance of it, if there is any at all. Maybe it was simply bought as a means to fill the space. Or maybe there's something deeper to the mass and accommodation it provides. Something that gives yet more insight into how tragically lonely this man who is blessed with so much, really is. How deeply he craves company and comfort. How tragically he craves human connection.

My mind clings to the questions, clawing at them for answers I have no business wanting about my boss.

But the fact he's paying me for human company has struck me with a sadness I can't seem to shake.

"Does it meet your approval?" I flinch at the sound of his deep voice, spinning to find him leaning his large body into the wall, dark eyes pinned unshakably to me.

I'm struck again by how darkly attractive he is. In a full black suit, his wavy dark hair is free from the tie he wears when he paints. The strands touch his shoulders in a way that would set Dad off on a spiel about his disappointment and disgust in men's fashion in the twenty-first century. He's shoved his big hands lazily into his pockets, but there's nothing truly lazy about his stance. The man emanates power.

"I—I'm sorry. I called and there was no answer." I swear, my face is seconds from bursting into the same flames that ring this building every night, igniting the sky in what the people call the fire of Hades.

His eyes don't waver from me as he pushes from the wall. In fact, his gaze feels even more intense as he prowls forward. Something inside me quivers, because until this very moment, I've never before felt as though I were the prey.

I think I might like it.

He stops when only inches separate us. "Persephone, while you are here, I want for you to feel as though you are home. Please, make my space your space. You are welcome to everything inside my home, to explore every space, outside my office and painting studio." He pauses as my heart beats so loud between us, it would be a marvel if he couldn't hear it. "My only ask, my only rule, is that you do not enter my office or studio without me being there. There are both priceless and," he clears his throat, but the crackle of danger remains. "Dangerous things in there."

"I won't invade your personal space, Mr. Pluton," I assure, but I feel robbed of breath as I do it. I can't quite put my finger on what it is about this man that affects me in a way no other does.

His serious expression cracks with a grin that touches on exasperation. He gives his head a small shake, and commands roughly, "Hades, Persephone. You will call me Hades."

"Of course." *God, I'm breathless.* Every sense I possess is alive.

"Now that's settled, shall I show you your room?"

"My room?" My brain is lagging, unable to keep up with this dynamic man.

"Yes, Persephone, your room." He quirks that grin at me. The one that promises threat in the delivery of a tease. "Unless you wish to share mine."

My heart skitters to a full stop. I'm positive the synapses in my brain sizzle, because for a moment, I am unable to form coherent thought. Then, blushing, I lift my chin. "My room, please."

He chuckles, but places his hand on my lower back. The gesture isn't in any way inappropriate or invasive, and yet my body heats to a near boiling point.

"Come, your room is across the hall from mine."

CHAPTER
TWELVE

P*ersephone*

THE ROOM HADES leads me to is nothing like the rest of his home. It's nothing like I imagine a bedroom in Greece to be like. It's nothing like the white room with the carved nooks in the walls that I share with Willa. The walls aren't painted a storm-gray, but instead a soft, warm, sandy beige. White wainscoting delivers a richly delicate welcoming that the rest of his home does not convey. The gold metal bedframe, with all its artful twists of vines and leaves is, a statement smack in the centre of the very large room. Draped across the mattress, is a plush green blanket of soft green threaded with delicate, and sparse gold roses. A cloud of pillows tops the head of the bed, and my bones instantly attempt to liquify with the need to sink into all that comfort.

I shake off the urge and let my eyes slide to the matching blush pink lamps that perch on mismatched white bedside tables. A cream-colored desk with a rose-pink chair sits to one side of the floor-to-ceiling window, while a bookshelf packed with books on Greek lore stands to the other side. A chaise chair in a pink so soft it almost looks white, sprawls over a very lightly tinted green carpet. The chandelier that hangs above it all appears to be dripping gold.

"There is a bathroom through that door." My gaze shifts to the door he gestures to. "And a closet through that one."

I feel suddenly, unexplainably, terribly unworthy.

Stiltedly, I turn to him. "Hades, this is—it's—"

"Everything you deserve." His voice is quiet, and unlike all the other people in my life, there is something about this man that makes me think he has some kind of gifted insight when it comes to my most secret, shameful thoughts. Or maybe it's not some paranormal gift he possesses, but simply that he pays attention. He sees. *He bothers to see.*

I shake my head. My voice comes out softer than I intend. There is a slightly wounded ring to my refusal. "It's too much."

He disregards my words with a dip of his eyes to

the small bag I carry. His voice, like him, is the rough to my soft. "Is that all you brought?"

I nod. My throat feels so dry. "Yes."

He frowns. "Do you intend to pack your outfit for the next day every day, Persephone? You are to spend six days a week here. You need more than a night bag."

I wet my dry lips, refusing to think about the way my blood warms as his eyes chase the movement. "I have four outfits here. I left five at the room I'm keeping in the house with the other students. That's all I have."

His eyes move up and down the length of my body, as though searing every dip and curve to memory before he says, "Unpack. Get settled and meet me in the kitchen."

With nothing more, he turns and exits the room.

Even when he's gone, I still can't quite catch my breath.

Everything—my whole life—feels suddenly surreal.

The shrill sound of my phone ringing snaps me out of my dazed contemplation of the twist my life has taken. I pull it from my pocket with shaking hands. Mom's contact lights up my screen in an invitation for FaceTime that has my insides twisting violently with nerves.

I can't answer here. This room is obviously nothing which I can afford, and I'm not ready to answer her questions. If Dad found out I was living with a man—

giving him company, cooking him meals, and sleeping in his home in exchange for payment—he'd be on the next flight.

I let the call run its course and then turn my phone off.

Unpacking only takes a minute, and the closet is entirely too large for the few measly outfits I have. I feel ridiculous as I hang them in the sprawling closet that is, I hate to admit, bigger than the room I have at home in Alberta.

I don't bother with makeup while working during the day, because I'm constantly reapplying sunscreen, and I'm not trying to impress anyone. So, I don't have to think about that as I splash cool water over my face, dabbing it dry with the softest towel I've ever touched. It's really true when they say rich people live different.

Everything feels so different here. My senses are somehow both soothed and stimulated. Everything is so beautiful and pleasant to the touch.

I can't help but think it's going to be difficult when September comes, and I'm sitting coach as I travel home to my closet-sized room with the normal, tough from one too many washes, towels.

I FIND Hades in the kitchen, pouring two glasses of crisp champagne. I know it's champagne by the little bubbles that dance inside the glass. He's removed his suit jacket and unbuttoned the first few buttons of his black shirt, rolling the sleeves up forearms that ripple with muscle under tan skin.

Good God, and I thought he couldn't get any hotter.

His lips twitch, but it's faint. "Do you like champagne?"

"I have the few times I've had it." He raises a brow in question that I answer, "I don't drink much." I smile with a huff of laughter. "I don't really drink at all, actually."

"I like a glass with dinner."

"I'll remember that." I take the glass he offers me as my eyes slide to the kitchen beyond him. "Speaking of dinner—what kind of foods do you like?"

"I'm not picky."

I frown. "That's not helpful."

He takes a swallow of the champagne, his penetrating eyes coming to me. "I will like anything you make for me, Persephone."

"You really should call me Annie. Everyone else does."

"I like Persephone."

I pull in breath. My odd name isn't a hill to die on. "Is there anything you *don't* like?"

He considers, and then he shakes his head. "No."

I tease, "So, I can make you grilled cheese and chicken nuggets in the shape of dinosaurs, and you're telling me you'll be happy?"

"I won't complain," he says with sincerity. "As long

as you promise they really will be in the shape of dinosaurs."

I laugh. It bursts from me entirely unexpected, because I did *not* expect his reply. "You can't be serious."

In all seriousness, he says, "I would never joke about dinosaur nuggets."

"You're handsome, wealthy, and funny," I observe. "You're the whole package, Hades, so why are you hiring me?"

His mouth turns up at one corner. "You think I'm handsome?"

"You know you are." *Why do I feel so breathless?*

That light in his eye turns devilishly dark. "What matters is that you think I am."

I push. "Why did you hire me, Hades? There has to be so many women throwing themselves at you all the time."

"Maybe that's why I hired you."

I cock my head, confused. "Sorry?"

"You have yet to throw yourself at me."

So, I was right. He feels wanted for little more than the things he can offer, not the man he is beyond the riches he can provide.

"If I threw myself at you?"

His voice drops to a rough kind of dark that strokes against the very core of me like a physical touch. "I would be hard pressed not to take you. To corrupt you. Completely."

My breath stalls in my lungs. Oh, who am I kidding, I'm not breathing at all. He's stripped me of breath with only one sentence. He's tossed a match to the embers of me with only one dark look.

I really shouldn't, but I can't help myself. "It doesn't bother you?"

"What?"

"That I'm so much younger than you."

His eyes drag the length of me, blazing the fire inside me even hotter. "Should it?"

"Probably."

He takes another drink. "You are a woman. Young, sure, but a woman all the same. And I am a man. If you invited, I wouldn't deny."

"Oh, wow." I breathe breathlessly. I clutch the glass between my hands, willing some of the chill to fan the flames inside me. "I—I—I don't know what to say."

"Persephone," he calls. I can't look at him. He rounds the island. He stops so close to me; I can smell the dark scent of him mixing with the sweet explosion that is the champagne in my glass. He commands, "Look at me."

I suck in a shuddering breath and squeeze my eyes closed. I feel ridiculous, but I'm shaking. Quaking down to the very bone. I started this inappropriate conversation with unintended consequences, and now I'm reaping those consequences. Because I *can't* look at him.

I've never felt fear like this.

"I am going to touch you," he warns, and then finger and thumb connect with my chin, tipping my head back. My eyes flutter open entirely of their own accord. I'm hit with the fullness of the dark attraction he exudes.

"Hades." His name is a tumble of overstimulated, raw nerves between us. I can't think.

"I've made you uncomfortable."

I shake my head. Then I nod. Then I murmur, "I don't know. I've never been like this with a man."

"Like what?"

"Alone like this. In a man's home. Trying to learn him." *Why does this feel so intimate?* "What he likes and doesn't like. What he expects from me." He is still holding my chin, keeping my eyes. I don't tell him he doesn't have to do that. I've been ensnared by his coal black gaze. There is nowhere else I can look. "I don't know what you expect from me—from this."

"Exactly what you have given me. Natural conversation."

"I don't want to do something that might," I stutter. "Lead you on."

His dark eyes darken, but he chuckles, releasing my chin. "Natural conversation often results in light flirting."

Is that what we'd been doing? Flirting?

"Oh."

"I will endeavor to be honest with you in all that I

can. I am a man entirely capable of engaging in light flirtation without physical expectation."

My face couldn't possibly be hotter. All I can manage is a pathetic, "Okay."

He holds my gaze. "This is why I've hired you." I'm confused, and it must show, because he continues, "Talking to you makes me feel like I can breathe. You don't feed me what you think I want to hear. You don't show me what you think I want to see. You are natural and refreshing and innocently unexpected." His lips quirk. "And I very much look forward to your dinosaur nuggets."

CHAPTER
THIRTEEN

P *ersephone*

I THOUGHT I'd toss and turn all night long my first night in Hades' home, but nope. I'd slept like the dead, waking only to the alarm I'd set for myself the night before. I dressed quickly before landing in the kitchen, prepared to make Hades breakfast, as per my job description, only to find a handwritten note on the counter. Hades explained that something pressing had come up, and he'd had to leave to take care of it.

He signed the note with: *See you tonight, Hades.*

I made myself a coffee and inspected his kitchen with the eye of a homicide detective. With the extra time I had in my morning since I wasn't cooking breakfast for Hades, I forewent the taxi and walked to the little house I shared with my team.

Now, after a long day spent under a brutally, but decadently hot sun, and a long walk to the Tower, I'm exhausted. I want nothing more than to wash away the day under a cool shower, and fall into that lovely bed. Still, even though I'm exhausted in a bone-deep way, I can't deny that I'm excited to cook for Hades.

I'm excited to see him.

Sometime during the day, I decided I'd make chicken and broccoli quesadillas. Hades had all the ingredients apart from the wraps, but I stopped in at a little grocer on the way to his home and bought a pack.

Now, as I ride the elevator to Hades' home, I feel even more nervous than I had the night before. After our borderline inappropriate conversation, thanks to yours truly, Hades insisted on ordering in for the night so that I could get comfortable. I'd tried to explain that cooking would make me more comfortable, but he wouldn't hear it. We shared takeout at the dining table, a second glass of champagne, which definitely went to my head, upon which I thought it smart to excuse myself for the night.

The elevator slides open and a quick jitter of nerves spike something that feels like fear in my heart. I swallow it down, and enter the space only to find myself facing off with three ferocious looking rottweilers.

It takes me a solid minute to realize that none of

the dogs are growling, or even looking at me with menace. Instead, apart from the middle one that stands, they don't even look all that threatening. The side two flank the middle, both sitting regally. Although I can see that they are well behaved, I can't ignore the sense that these dogs could rip a foe into shreds in only a matter of seconds.

The thought has pebbles of fear rising over every inch of my skin, before Hades appears, his dark eyes taking in the scene and my fear before he commands, "Beds."

All three dogs turn and walk slowly, unwillingly, away.

Nerves spill from my lips in a telling laugh as I breathe, "You have dogs."

His eyes narrow. "You don't like dogs?"

"I like dogs. Love them, actually." I kick off my shoes, reveling in the feel of his cool floor on my hot feet. "But I walked into their home with no introduction. The fact I like dogs wouldn't stop them from seeing me as a threat to their space and master, and potentially ripping me apart."

"They will never harm you."

I frown at the man, because he should know better than that. They are animals, and I've not been properly introduced. They could have ended me before Hades even blinked just now.

I sigh heavily, because Hades struck me as more intelligent than that. "Hades, they don't know me."

"I've introduced your scent to them. They know you are not to be harmed."

"My scent?" I feel my brows rise to my hairline. Sometimes, this man is bizarre.

"I let them into your room. They know you are to be protected, never harmed." His eyes bore into mine. "Persephone, they understand."

There it is again. His odd ability to climb into my mind and read my thoughts.

I just shake my head, at a loss. Lifting the bag of tortillas, I tell him, "I'm going to get dinner started."

His jaw hardens. My eyes widen. "I don't want you spending money on things for my home."

I brush him off. "It's nothing."

"Persephone." There is a warning in his tone that has me pausing. "I'm serious. If you want something that I don't have, write it down and I'll have my housekeeper pick it up."

I consider arguing, but when it boils down, I am *his* employee. I don't want to be fired on day two for insubordination. Reluctantly, I nod. Slipping around him, I move into the kitchen. I don't miss the three massive dog beds that line the wall in the living room, or the massive dogs that rest in each bed.

Still, Hades says they won't harm me, and I decide to trust him. I'll make friends with the pups soon enough.

"I hope everything was okay today." I pull chicken, cheese, and broccoli from the fridge. When Hades says nothing, I peek up at him to find he's looking at me with an adorably confused expression on his face. I almost laugh, but thankfully keep it contained as I explain, "You said you had something pressing come up in your note." I think maybe I shouldn't have asked, but the man basically said he was looking for a wife, without the bedroom bits. I figure a wife would press, so I do, too. "It was just a little early for something pressing to have happened." I shrug as I tear into the pack of chicken. "I worried about you today, is all."

"You worried about me?"

God, why is it that his voice affects me like this? Like it physically climbs inside my body and flips all my switches.

Hades cocks his head, eyes darkening as I wet my lips. "Of course, I did."

He tosses a big hand toward the dogs. "Them."

My brows inch together. "What?"

"The pressing thing I had to see to was them. My dogs."

"Oh." My eyes slide to the big pups, and I give them a soft smile. Living on a farm my whole life, we'd had dogs. Plenty of dogs. But I'd lost my most favorite less than six months ago to old age, and the pain of that loss still hurts. "Where were they?"

"At my other home."

My furrowed brows inch high. "You have another home?"

Hades nods. "I do."

"Wow." I slice the cut chicken from the cutting

board into a pan. With a new board, I begin chopping the broccoli. "What does a man need two homes for?"

"My other home is my true home," he says. "This home is simply convenient."

I snort. "Feels more like paradise to me."

"Does it?"

I glance around at the opulence. "I mean, yeah."

"This is what you want, Persephone? What your soul craves?" He raises a single brow. "Is that what you're telling me?"

His mention of my soul stirs something inside of me. It's the same something that stirs when I hear that voice that calls my name, with all its rage and anguish. My tongue feels dry. "I'm not sure what you're asking, Hades."

"If you could, would you choose to live here for the rest of your life?"

There's something intense about his expression that I can't quite put my finger on. I feel, oddly, like this is a test. Still, I don't want to offend him when it comes to the place he's obviously chosen to live, even if he has another home elsewhere that he prefers more.

I begin cautiously. "I don't know that I would refuse it, if it was offered to me. But if I could choose anything at all—then, no, this wouldn't be it."

"If you could choose anything at all, what would it be?"

My lips part and close and part again. "I—I don't know."

I don't know why this question feels so intimate. It's a basic question that anyone could ask, and yet it feels—like a lot.

"Persephone," Hades calls, and I see that he's moved closer when I peek from the cut broccoli to him. "Please, tell me."

"I don't know that I would choose to be so close to the sky. It feels—I feel a little out of place. Itchy in my own skin, I think. Even though it's very beautiful here. The view." The words come out of nowhere. Until this very moment, I hadn't even realized I felt this way. But with the words between us, I can't deny the truth of them. "And it's very modern. I feel it's lacking, well, life."

When I dare to look at him, I find it odd that he looks almost pleased.

The man is peculiar.

FOURTEEN

H *ades*

PERSEPHONE WASN'T LYING when she said she could cook. She also wasn't lying when she said she enjoys cooking. It's clear she's comfortable in the kitchen, and to my relief, she mostly uses natural ingredients. Having lived for millennia, I can attest to the fact that life for humanity has become exponentially easier, and exponentially lazier. For the most part, I very much dislike the food in the middle realm. It's filled with chemicals intended to preserve the food, while killing the consumer. The number of souls I've condemned to Tartarus that work in the food business, knowingly poisoning innocent consumers for riches, is ever-growing and despicable.

Swallowing another dill and lemon seasoned potato, I allow my eyes to slide back to her. I've come to notice that she grows uncomfortable if I allow my gaze to linger on her for lengthy times, and expend conscious effort to keep from drinking in every part of her, every moment she spends with me. If I looked at only her for the rest of my eternity, I can't say I would not be blessed.

She stirs life inside of me. She awakens the parts of me that have been dying since she was stolen, gruesomely taken from me in an act that weaved the web of destruction that would follow in the centuries to come.

When I returned to the Underworld to retrieve Cerberus, Hecate had informed me, that for the first time in the last century, the stars had stopped falling. The Tree of Life in the Elysium Fields, not only stopped shedding leaves, but began to bud again.

A new bud has not been observed since the Day of Death in the Underworld, where the one truly living thing—the one thing with a soul bound to life and not death—had been violently, brutally, betrayed. Murdered.

Stolen.

The food sours in my mouth at the memory, and I push my plate away.

The way I raged in the past when the memory of

Persephone bound beneath the waters of The Lethe, her dark green eyes wide in death—it had been intense. My grief had shaken the Underworld so fiercely, that the earth itself trembled. Land split, allowing Poseidon to circle the land he did not swallow in his seas. Lives were lost, souls claimed.

Atlantis had fallen.

"Is everything all right?"

I blink the fire from my gaze, dipping my eyes to the obsidian gloss of the table. It takes a moment, but the magma of Tartarus in my veins slows its flow, cooling.

"Yes." My voice sounds rough even to my own ears.

She shifts across the table from me. Awareness slithers through the valves of my heart, Medusa's serpents rooting precariously in the depths of the organ that beats exclusively, dangerously, for the oblivious little woman who holds the soul of my mate in her fragile human body. This chance I have with her now, I know without even visiting the *Moirai,* The Fates, is the last chance I will be given with her soul. If she is taken from me again, the heart inside my eternal chest will, undoubtedly turn to stone, trapped within a grief I will never recover from. The Underworld will collapse. The prisons of the Titans, bound by my blood, will fail. Freeing the beginning of what will be the end of all that has ever been known.

She touches me, and I breathe. Her hand is small against the stone of my shoulder. "Hades?"

"I'm fine."

"You don't look fine."

I grind my teeth, keeping my head bowed as I tighten the reigns of my splintering control. If she knew the way I burned when she touched me, she would not do it. And yet, I don't want her to stop.

I want to loose the God that claws at the flesh of the man that contains him, and claim her. I want to swallow her screams and cries. To play the chords of her unwilling pleasure until she gifts me with the moans I ache to devour. I want to shove inside her body, to claim her innocence and ravage the purity of her warm heart, consuming the whole of her for my own so that I may never lose her again.

I want her soul. The God within rages for it, willing to steal to possess it. Whatever the cost.

But the man knows better. The man has lived in this human form for centuries, shoving at the consuming grief of the God that threatens to overwhelm him.

Her hand moves over my back, and the God hums his approval.

If she knew the way she affected me with just this simple contact, how the threads of her freedom frayed under her friendly comfort, she would certainly flee me.

"I had a rough day." With a scrub of my hands over my face, I lift my now cool gaze to hers. "I apologize."

Her full mouth shifts into a soft, innocently caring smile. I ache to taste it.

"Would you like to talk about it?"

Would I like to tell her that the continuation of the Underworld, the Middle World, The Oceans, and even the golden expanse of Olympus, is tied to her willingness to deliver me her soul? No. No, I would not.

Slowly, I shake my head. I note the disappointment that shadows her lovely green eyes, like emeralds mined from the riches of the earth, and ask instead, "Are you tired?"

She sucks her lower lip. *I've never been more jealous in my life.* Her voice is soft. "No."

I have to clear my throat. "Will you join me this evening, then?"

Caution battles the shadows in her eyes. "Where?"

"On the rooftop." I add when she hesitates, "For conversation."

Her eyes flick to the ceiling, full lips parting.

Fuck, but I ache to cover her mouth with my own. If she weren't so skittish about the gap in our age, I might have done it already. But she is skittish. She's overly prudish in her unwillingness to act in a way that goes against the appropriateness of our restrictive rolls as employer and employee. I am confident all this is owed to the web Demeter weaved into the curse she cast on our great love.

She took her case to the Fates centuries past. She

claimed that together our power was too vast, too much, too unchecked and dangerous.

There must have been some truth to that which she claimed, because the Fates acted. They weaved. And the fate they weaved was the thing that punished us for too long.

I am reminded, yet again, that I must visit the *Moirai*. Yet the very thought leaves my flesh feeling chilled, unease icing the very bones beneath my skin. For the webs the Fates weave is never in black and white. And Fate, even written, is ever-evolving.

Their riddles, even for a God, are spun in threads lacking transparency and dipped in the rivers that flow from the Three Mountains that overlook the Underworld, ruling like overlords in a realm that is entirely their own. For the Three Mountains in the Underworld are only the base of what is known above as Mount Olympus. Incorrectly, from the dregs of an ancient myth, it is presumed Mount Olympus is the home of the Gods. Instead, it is the passage of the *Moirai*. The heart of all that is. Her roots so deep they sew into the earth of the Underworld, so wide her skeleton stretches into the sea, so vast she plunges into the sky. It is a realm unto itself, the home of the Fates, tying all that is and all that has been or will ever be, together as one.

For the most part, I leave the *Moirai* to themselves, as do the other Gods. Not even the Gods wish to command their scrutiny. Look what has come of me under their disassociated ire. The punishment I suffered for daring to command the rare and coveted power of true love.

Persephone's hand falls from my shoulder, calling my thoughts back to the present. To her.

Confusion knots her brow, and I ache to wipe it tenderly away. To give her words of assurance.

I need to find a way to break through her barriers. To make the want she already feels for me, even at her denial, too strong to refuse.

Our time is limited, and passing quickly. Every second that passes, the danger she is in increases. *I must claim her living soul.*

I force a smile to my lips, watching as her eyes drop and her full breasts rise with her inhale. Then she whispers, "Let me tidy this up and I'll join you." More to herself than me, she repeats, "For conversation."

FIFTEEN

P*ersephone*

SOMETHING IS UP WITH HADES. I've only worked for him for a week, but I can tell that something isn't right. Most nights, we sit at the table and talk about lots of nothing. Hades likes to hear about my uneventful life as a farmer's daughter, which, after four nights together, I swear he knows inside and out. I've come to note that he loves his dogs deeply, which makes him feel more human and less—*massive*—to me.

His boy and two girls, I've come to realize, are big teddy bears. They are named after the night and his night blooming flowers, which I find entirely too endearing. The boy, Nocturnum, is always between his girls, Jasmine and Primrose. Hades calls them Noc, Jas, and Prim, and as such, do I.

It doesn't take me long to clean up after dinner, packaging the left-over grilled fish into a container for tomorrow's lunch. I feel strung with nerves at the thought of spending my first full day with Hades tomorrow, leaving for my one night at the house with my friends on Sunday. I'd considered asking for Saturday to be my free night, but since I don't enjoy clubbing, which is a big Saturday thing with the others in my program, Sunday better suits my day off all around.

"Can I pour you a glass?" I shift to find Hades with a bottle of red wine in his hand.

I push the towel I'm drying my hands off on into the rail on the oven, and ask, "Are you trying to turn me into a lush, Hades?"

He arches one brow. "Hardly."

"You're always offering me a drink."

"Only with meals."

"And now, too." I gesture at the bottle. Since our first night, when I felt the wine we'd indulged in after dinner sway the rational flow of my thoughts, I'd been cautious about sticking to tea in the evenings.

His lips quirk, and something lightens the shadows that swirl in his eyes. The shadows have been there since he got quiet over dinner, and whatever it was that happened to him during the day sucked his thoughts into a dark vortex that

shifted his easy mood from comfortable to dangerous, fast.

"You are off tomorrow. I thought maybe you'd
like to let loose a little." He swirls the bottle.
"Have a glass or two of wine with me, Persephone," he dares, his voice dropping to a
dangerous pitch that instantly pulls an unwilling,
and dangerously sharp response from the depths
of my core. I shift, squeezing my legs together in a
way I desperately pray is imperceptible. I think,
maybe I've failed, when his eyes snap to mine,
dipping low and dragging hotly over the length of
me. His nostrils flare and his throat works with a
hard swallow.

Run. The word is shrill in my mind. A voice that is
not my own, and I am helpless to obey.

I am rooted to the floor.

Fear and something else, something I think terrifyingly might be arousal, thrums an intoxicatingly
unwelcome tune within my body.

"Hades," I breathe, shuddering.

His eyes snap to mine and I swear, I see flames
dancing in the depths.

What the hell?

He shutters his eyes, and when they open again,
the fire is gone. A mirage, I decide, of the heat that
simmers in my own core.

His voice is rough, like thrown gravel as he dares
again, "Have a glass with me, Persephone. I vow to

you; your virtue is safe with me." There is a pause, before he adds, "For tonight."

I think his words are supposed to assure me, but instead, I can't help but read the underlying promise within them. The delicious threat. The dark assurance that it's only a matter of time before this man devours my virtue, corrupting all of me until I'm so wound up in the darkness of him, I won't be able to unthread the knots we foolishly weave.

When I fail to agree, he simply pours the wine into two glasses. "There is a pool on the rooftop. Why don't you go get changed into a swimsuit?" His dark eyes dance. "Join me for a swim?"

Wait, the man has a pool on the roof!? I manage, "I don't have a swimsuit."

"Yes, you do."

I frown, because I know the meager items I packed. The massive closet in the room Hades provided for me make my lack of personal possessions all the more glaringly obvious.

I shake my head. "I only have the four outfits, Hades. This——" I gesture down at what I'm wearing. "Is the last outfit I have. I'll need to do my laundry tomorrow before I get dressed."

I really should have done my laundry last night. But I'd been so tired after spending time with Hades after dinner, I'd fallen into bed and slept, as I'd been sleeping every night in the bed Hades provided for me, like the dead.

"Maya did your laundry this morning, along with the clothing I had delivered for you today."

"You—" I stutter, swallowing hard. "You had clothing delivered for me?"

"I did." He takes a slow sip of his wine.

"Why?"

"Why not?"

"Because..." I grasp for words. "It's expensive."

His lips twitch. "Hmm."

"Hades." I drop my hands onto my hips. "You can't go around spending money on me."

His voice drops to a low and dangerous warning. "I can do whatever I wish, Persephone."

I ignore the warning. "Not when it comes to me, you can't."

That damn brow arcs. "Is that a dare?"

"It's a command!" I huff. "I don't want you spending money on me. It's pointless and—and it makes me feel..."

He pushes away from the counter to take dangerous steps closer. "What does it make you feel?"

"I don't k-know," I stammer, hating that I do.

After a long pause, Hades says softly, "You deserve everything this world has to give. I am not only able to give it to you, but I want to give it to you."

Searching the dark pools of his eyes, I feel so terribly fragile. "Hades, I'm your employee."

"You are a beautiful young woman, and I am an affected man."

My skin heats. "That's not what we are."

How does he always make me so hot?

He cocks his head slightly to the side. "I am aware of exactly what we are. Now, be a good girl and do as you're told, as a good employee should, and get changed."

There is a lot to unpack in his single command. I could dismantle it time and again and still have more to unravel in the aftershocks of the feelings his words strike inside me.

But I don't dismantle it, because then I'll have to face those aftershocks. I'm not ready for that, so without another word, I spin on my heel and leave for my room with the three pups following close on my heel.

SIXTEEN

P *ersephone*

I HOLD my door open as Noc, Jas, and Prim strut through. When it falls with a soft *click*, and I flinch, three sets of eyes fall on me as though to ask, *what?*

They might be Hades' dogs, but they've taken to wanting to be with me. At first, it made me uncomfortable and nervous that *his* dogs he very clearly loves very dearly, would choose me over him. But now, I suspect that Hades not only prefers them to remain with me, but that he's commanded it and they somehow understand him enough to listen to such a bizarre command.

Noc remains at his station by the bedroom door,

which is always his station while the girls follow me to the closet. Jas sits outside, but Prim dances into the room with me, her eyes watchful as I feel my belly sink into my feet.

Hades didn't just buy a few things. He bought enough to completely fill the big closet.

My mouth drops at the section of work clothes. They're all light in color to keep me from overheating under the hot sun I've begun to crave more and more every day while I dig, shifting to the relaxed section of at-home wear that is comfortable, but still stylish. I see jeans, suit pants and leggings, shorts, skirts, and summer dresses all to be paired with shirts of all kinds, cardigans, sweaters, and jackets. There is also an enormous, and quite frankly silly, section of gowns the kind of elegant that I can't imagine I will ever have reason to wear.

Numbly, I pull open the drawers to see underwear, night dresses and lingerie, swimsuits, scarves, and accessories. There are rows of shoes for every occasion.

"The man is a nutcase," I breathe to myself, but from the corner of my eye, I see Prim's head cock to the side. "Even more than I am." I touch a gown that glimmers like starlight in the night sky. "He's a madman."

Prim gives a doggy huff. I'm not quite sure if it's in agreement, or not. It doesn't matter, though. Hades *is* clearly a few marbles short of sane if he's willing to spend this kind of money on his hired companion.

But I can't deny it all makes me feel special. Like I am more to him than I am or can ever be.

Feeling frazzled and wanting to escape this closet, I grab the first swimsuit I see and start to strip. When the suit is pulled into place, I can't help but gape at myself in the mirror. I've always worn one-piece suits, but Hades hasn't given the option of anything but bikinis in the drawer of suits.

Midnight black clings to my skin with features of gold that warm the paleness of my skin. With my wavy, white-blonde hair, I feel like I look a little mythical. A lot unlike the girl I've always known myself to be. But that's the magic of Hades. He always makes me feel different. More. Right from that very first moment when I opened my mouth and spilled my innermost secret to him.

Pushing the thoughts from my mind, I find a sheer black cover and slide it on. I tie it tight at my waist, grab a towel and hurry from the room.

To the side of the kitchen, I find an open door that has always been locked. It's open wide now, displaying a wide set of stairs to another door that is also open wide. The sky above is painted in strokes of midnight, shimmering with a million dotted stars. Like someone tossed glitter onto a canvas of black to bring it alive.

It's so big, so vast, and should be so heavy. But rather than crush me with its great expanse, I feel as though something is lifted from my chest. My insecurities, maybe?

I pull my gaze from the sky to find an oasis of pleasure. There is a long glittering pool of blue with water so still under the open sky, I can almost see the faint twinkle of the starlight in the glass of it.

My gaze slides beyond the pool to the other side of the rooftop paradise, where there is a massive shelter done in rich wood tones. The top is painted a crisp, bright white to ward off a high dramatic sun. Little bulbs illuminated with warm amber light string from the rafters over an intimate hot tub, seating area, and bar. Lush plants sit in massive pots, bringing life to an otherwise stark but luxurious space.

My eyes drift from the lights back to the pool, landing on Hades. My heart skitters and my breath stalls. Tingles of awareness erupt over my skin, and my mouth goes bone dry.

The man is—there are no words.

But if I had to find words, I would say he is massively dark and dangerously, devilishly handsome. I haven't seen his chest bare since the interview when Leuce led me to the room where he was painting. The effect now is as damning as it was then.

But his eyes—his dark eyes are what have me rooted to the ground, struck still by the physical touch of his gaze.

"Come," he says roughly from the opposite side of

the pool. He is facing me, his arms thrown up over the ledge as one might toss them over the back of a couch. "Join me."

Clearing my throat, I move closer on legs that feel wobbly. My knees are crafted of jelly. Unable to handle standing when he looks at me like he is, I try to save face and lower myself to sit on the edge of the pool. I dip my feet into cool water that seems to sear my boiling blood, offering tiny relief.

It's delicious, but I feel only a little of the tension seeping from my flesh. The rest clings to me as though it is a thing of claws and teeth, hungering for the flesh of me.

Needing to say something, anything—to simply fill the space with something other than this new need he's pulling from the depths of me, I murmur, "This is beautiful, Hades."

"I rarely take the time to enjoy it."

From the corner of my eye, I see the pups sprawling on the stone of the patio, cooled gently by a high moon.

"Why?"

"I am a busy man, Persephone."

I blush, because he *is* a busy man. As the owner of a highly successful club and an artist, of course, he is busy. I feel foolish.

Still, I tell him, "You only get one life. You should live it."

There's a pull of amusement to the lips he rolls

before he murmurs, "How can you be so sure there is only one life?"

I shrug, kicking my feet gently in the water. "That's what everyone says. Do you believe we live multiple lives?"

Somehow, I can't see it. This powerful man believing a thought so fanciful that there is anything more than *this*.

He surprises me. "I believe humans live as many lives as they choose to live."

"Humans." I frown. "That's a peculiar distinction."

He doesn't reply. Not physically with a shrug or verbally with words. But his eyes say so many things. They speak a language I'm not sure I understand, but my body shivers all the same, sensing something my mind can't form into words.

He commands, "Come inside, Persephone."

What is it about the man's commands that I am helpless to refuse? What about them makes me want to comply?

Severing my gaze from his, my hands move to the tie I've knotted at my waist. I realize, to my absolute horror, that my knees aren't the only thing that has turned to jelly. My fingers tremble, slipping over the knot as panic builds inside me.

Hades pushes from the wall to plunge into the water, looking like a predator from the depths of a dark sea. He swims the length of the pool to the shallow end where I sit, his body splicing through the blue with a power that lashes at my awareness. He rises and water drips from his longish hair, glistening on his wide, carved chest as he prowls across the space I've very strategically kept between us.

Inside my chest my heart slams. This time, my breaths don't stall in my lungs. Instead, they race from me in short, quick bursts.

"What are you..." My words drift off in shock as the feel of his big hot hands land on my thighs, spreading my legs wide enough for the bulk of him to move between.

Heat unlike any other I've ever experienced before this moment surges through me. My sudden sharp arousal is an eruption of magma in my veins. It pools like a lake in my very core, filling the hollow of me with an aching need fiercer than any other. It steals my breath and sensibility.

I've never had a man so close to me. I've never had a man touch me as Hades touches me.

A spill of wet rushes from between my legs to settle sticky in my bathing suit as I imagine Hades' big hands sliding higher up my thighs to touch me *there*. To stroke me. To invade me.

I very nearly whimper as my core clenches hard again. *God, I'm wet for him.*

Hades' nostrils flare, and I swear I see that fire flash in his eyes before he shutters them again. His hands move to the tie at my waist, gently shoving mine away. He rumbles, "Let me."

Hades makes quick work of the knot, and the sheer black material parts to showcase pale skin kissed in moonlight, and the black bikini. A sharp inhale sounds and my eyes spear to his as he lifts his hands to my shoulders, pushing the material from my body, grazing my skin with hot fingertips as he does.

I shiver, pebbles of aching awareness rising on my skin. In the bikini, my breasts feel heavy and swollen. My nipples are painfully hard.

I pray he won't notice, and die a little when his eyes drop to my breasts. He wets his lips in an absent gesture that cries of a ravenous hunger I don't know how to sate, before his gaze drifts up to mine once again.

"You're cold." His voice is hoarse, clinging to ravaged control.

I'm not. I feel as though I'm a mere moment from bursting into flames. Still, the rough grate of his voice has another violent shiver pulsing through me.

I lie, "Yes."

Hades shifts to the side of me, pulling himself up from the pool before he reaches for my hand. I can't help the way my eyes linger on the drops of water that slide over the warm tones of his skin, between the valleys of muscle that ripple under his flesh.

He pulls me up to stand, and to my horror, my jelly knees fail me and my body slams into his. It's a collision of flame and sin and innocence. Woodsmoke swirls. He's so much bigger than me, I think, as his arm moves to band around the small of my back. He pins my softness to the wide, hard, hot expanse of his chest.

My thoughts fracture.

My heart flips in its cage. A whimpered breath spills from my lips as I steady myself with a hand to his breast. Under it, I can feel the rapid-fire dance of his quickening pulse.

God, what am I doing?

Hades swallows, and his voice sounds rough as he asks, "Good?"

I nod, pushing myself from his chest. "I'm sorry, I —I..."

"Tripped?" Hades provides for me and I nod, even though we both know it's more. "Let's get you into the hot tub so you can warm up."

Again, I nod, but I say nothing. I don't trust my voice right now. I don't trust my body or my emotions or this yawning hunger that is growing within me for something I can't allow myself to take.

I wonder if it's just Hades or if I let myself, I could feel this same want with Addison. He's impossibly attractive, and entirely opposite to Hades. He'd been flirting shamelessly with me all week long, but I hadn't reciprocated, even though I could admit his attention felt good. Sort of.

And Addison is *my* age.

Still, every time I think of flirting back with Addison, something ugly balloons inside me. Something that makes me feel hideous and wrong. Thoughts of Hades plague me in the moments I am away from him.

This crush is ridiculous and inappropriate. I need to get a handle on myself, like...yesterday.

I wish I knew what was happening to me. I wish I could explain away this wicked craving for my boss that I try so desperately to hide. To bury deep within me where not even I can find it.

He awakened something within me that first night we stood shoulder-to-shoulder, staring into the devastatingly captivating horror of his art. He spilled fuel to the spark of hunger his darkly intense gaze ignited within me, and I've been burning up ever since.

I don't want to admit it, but I can't refuse it either. I've tried.

I've lied to myself and to him, desperate to keep the lines between us sharp and clean.

Hades lowers into the bubbling water of the hot tub, gesturing for me to do the same. My knees knock as I shimmy to the ledge. Under his breath, Hades says something to himself as he reaches up to close his hot, hard hands around the small of my waist. I gasp a breath of still night air, as he lowers me into the water before him. I'm so close to him, I can smell the scent of woodsmoke and sin and cool, refreshing earth.

He removes his hands from my body, giving me the space I so desperately need before I'm incinerated by desire. He lifts a glass of wine from the ledge, passing it to me.

I take a deep drink of the dry red, praying for reprieve from the heat and devastated to realize it's only fueled the fire that rages in the depths of me. The heat of the wine is like spilled magma as it moves through my body, swimming into the desire that surges like a tremulous sea of fire and sin in my belly.

I need to get a handle on myself.

"I've been meaning to speak with you." Hades settles himself onto a seat, resting one arm over the ledge as the other lifts his own glass of wine.

"Oh?"

"You recall when I hired you, how I said I may require you to accompany me to functions?" I nod, but say nothing. He continues, "There is a gala at the end of the month in celebration of the opening of the new hospital we've built."

"You built a hospital?"

"Myself and some other large investors, yes." He watches me closely, and I struggle to keep from shifting under the heavy weight of his gaze. "This gala will help to fundraise once again, for the patients."

I nod. *That must be what all the gowns in the closet are for.* "You want me to come with you?"

"I do."

"As your assistant?"

He shakes his head. "As my date."

My lips part, and to help my cough go back the

way it came, I take another deep swallow of wine. "But —we can't—I'm not…"

He doesn't let me finish. "I am tired of these events, Persephone. Women eligible for marriage attend, attempting to hook their claws into men of stature and wealth by any means. It is exhausting fending them off time and again." He gives me a rueful grin. "I am asking that you accompany me as my date so that I do not have to fight quite as hard."

I'm not sure he's seeing the big picture. Cautiously, I ask, "You aren't concerned what people will say?"

"About what?"

"Hades," I say his name, exasperated. "I'm nineteen and you—you are thirty-six!"

He pauses. "How do you know I'm thirty-six?"

"Google."

He arcs that brow. "You Googled me?"

"Everyone Googles everyone," I huff.

He tips his head, only slightly, in thought. "When did you Google me?"

"When you hired me," I admit, blushing. "I was curious."

He is quiet for a moment. "Did you find what you were looking for?"

I wet my lips, considering. "Not really."

"And what was it you were looking for, Persephone?"

I shake my head slowly. "I—I'm not sure." I snap out of the spell he's put me under, and say tiredly, "I can't go with you, Hades. It will ruin your reputation."

"How so?"

"I already told you. I'm too young to be your date."

"You are nineteen, and will soon be twenty. In the eyes of the law, you are legal. How is that too young?"

I tip my head back to the sky, pleading for deliverance. When I look back to Hades, I find a smirk playing at the corners of his lips. "You are almost seventeen years older than me."

"Age is just a number." I make a noise, and he continues, "All that matters is we are two consenting adults."

"You're really willing to risk your whole reputation to avoid a night of women throwing themselves at you?"

"They really are vicious creatures," he says, but there's a mocking tease to it that has a reluctant smile pulling at my lips. "Say you will, Persephone."

"What exactly do you want from this, Hades? For me to simply be a barrier between you and the *vicious creatures*?"

He laughs, and it is—it affects me. In a way it shouldn't.

I shift in my seat, waiting.

He replies, "I want them to think that you are mine, and I am yours."

I feel my lips part. "But..."

"It doesn't have to be real." He sighs. "It simply must look real."

"Look real?"

"As though we are a couple."

I swallow my shock. "You want me to be your fake girlfriend?"

Darkly, with a touch of ominous amusement, he says, "For now."

CHAPTER
SEVENTEEN

 *ades*

THE WORK of the Fates truly is like no other. When they spin their wheel, weaving their threads, the crisscross of paths, the foresight, really, it is unparallelled. The webs are sticky and complex, and I should have known that when I was presented time and again with an option to sponsor the archeology program that brought Persephone here to Greece, to fund the passion that is the study of the ancient Gods, that this thread would be the one to lead her back to me.

I should have known, but I hadn't suspected a thing. I'd sponsored the program as a means to do what I've always done, bettering the lives of the people while raising awareness of the Gods they have forgotten. The Gods who hold the balance of their precious world in their palms. The Gods who are growing more and more tired, with every forgotten century that crawls by.

Imagine my surprise when I dug deep into what I know of Persephone's life, only to discover that she'd nearly emptied her personal savings in order to pay for this opportunity. The parents she speaks of so lovingly clearly hadn't supported her in this. If they had, they would have helped her to pay for this experience.

And how hadn't I noticed that a young woman named Persephone had registered? I had all the files here in my office the entire time. I could have been prepared for her—if I'd just read them.

But that's the thing about Fate. In all the webs she weaves, all the threads she pulls, there are still paths we can choose to take. There is still free will. And that is why Fate is ever-changing, always evolving.

"You won't believe who else is in the program." Minthe enters my office, dropping into the plush couch I keep in here for both her and Leuce.

I slide my eyes from the registration, where I've entered Minthe as a late entry even though she's been working the program close to Persephone for the last week.

"Don't keep me in suspense, Minthe."

"But I know you love suspense so much," she teases, the little nymph.

I sit back in my chair, giving her my gaze. It's what she wants, and I get confirmation of that fact when a slow smile curls her lips.

"Adonis."

Every muscle in my body tightens. My pitch drops, the death of my realm slipping into my tone. "Is that so?"

"Oh, it's so."

"How can you be so certain?"

"Hades," Minthe deadpans, but there's a spark of offense in her green eyes. "I've been around a long time. I know what a reincarnated soul looks like. Adonis is here, and he's determined to have Persephone for his own." A delicate laugh chimes between us. "Dare I say, he's almost as smitten as you."

Fucking Fates. "He was always taken with her."

"He's more than taken with her." Minthe settles into the cushions, the teasing glint to her eyes washing away with something more serious. Grave, even. "Hades, I am aware Adonis was and is human. But I believe..." She shifts on the couch, her hesitation clear. "I believe his soul remembers her."

"If his soul remembers her—"

She finishes when I pause. "Then his love for her was real. Pure and true."

"She is mine." The words sound on a growl. Low

and fierce and bursting with a deadly protectiveness that stems from an ancient possessiveness.

"I know," Minthe says placatingly. "I'm simply warning you."

"And her soul?" Anger vibrates in the dark tones of my demand. "Does her soul remember him?"

Minthe is quiet for a long moment as she considers. Against my thighs under my desk, my hands curl into fists capable of the greatest monstrosities.

I warn, "Minthe."

Minthe blinks. "I do not know, Hades. I am undecided."

"Why?" I demand, at the end of a very short fuse. "It is a simple question."

"Persephone's soul is—it's complex." Minthe's tone is as soft as her eyes. "She was drowned in the river Lethe, Hades—"

"I know how she was taken from me, Minthe," I growl low and dangerously. "I am the one who found her."

Minthe severs eye contact, submitting to the beast that crawls under the surface of my skin. An ancient and unforgiving God. A thing of nightmares and curses. I can feel him hovering below the surface of my flesh, my gaze burning with the urge to let him break free.

Minthe pulls in a deep breath, careful not to challenge the monster by raising her head and daring eye contact again, lest he slip free from the prison of my flesh to destroy all that she is. Her voice trembles. "Persephone is different, as we suspected. The Lethe took her memories, stripped her bare of them all—but she is a Goddess. Her core soul, even stripped, is eternal. There are pieces of her, shards of recognition, I think. Her soul has no real memory, but there is something there. I see it in the way she pauses sometimes, the way she struggles to process. I think—I think it might be like déjà-vu for her. She knows, but she doesn't."

"Explain."

"She was born as the daughter of a farmer in a small Alberta town, in a country far from our own. She has never travelled to Greece, and yet she yearned to be here so deeply, driven by a soul-deep need to travel here, to you. Only a God or Goddess would be able to retain something like that after being drowned by The Lethe." Quieter, her eyes still trained to the floor between us, she adds, "It only goes to show how powerful she really is."

Something hums in my blood. "Look at me, Minthe." She obeys instantly, without hesitation. "Explain."

"Drinking from The Lethe is not something a soul does lightly. For the souls who do dare to drink, it is never more than a taste. That's all it takes to strip a soul of its most core memories. The memories that shape it for the next life, the memories that give the soul an elevated edge to the playing field in a world that grows more and more complex with every life-time. The consequences are so massive, Hades, the souls who drink lose *intuition*. They lose the ability to read between the lines, to decipher the meaning of a hunch. They must relearn instinct in a world filled with souls who *do* remember. Whose souls have tiny recognitions from *all* the lives they've lived before. Souls who know places and people and the smell of danger or the taste of love."

She pulls in a breath. "Persephone did not simply drink from The Lethe, Hades. She was drowned in it. The water did not simply trickle down her throat into her belly, it filled her belly and burst her lungs." Emotion shimmers in Minthe's eyes. Her lips tremble with emotion as she whispers her next words, "It raped her soul. Yet her soul is so powerful, so prevailing, she has retained some of that instinct from which she should have been stripped. She may not remember as she might have had she not been submerged in The Lethe, violated by the rage of the river, but she remembers more than she should, considering the same."

"That's why Demeter did it." The realization comes to me in a wash of cold that threatens the heat of the ancient God beneath my skin.

How had I missed it before? The breadth of her power. It was never *our* power, as I had thought, that frightened the Fates enough to cut the thread of Perse-phone's life, her destiny. It was *her* power. My ego as a new and bloodthirsty God, relishing his might, had blinded me to the deadly reality my mate would face in consequence for the power she bestowed upon the world crafted by the Gods before her. A world she would *change*.

I've lived enough years to know that nothing sparks fear in the Gods quite like the threat of change, and those with the power to spark it. To craft it.

Minthe cocks her head. "What?"

"Her power. It's more than we thought—than I thought. But Demeter knew. Demeter created her, coveted her. She wanted to use her and when I took Persephone, I threatened her plans, whatever it is they were. When she fell in love with me, when I stole her heart as well as her body—Demeter lost the beast she intended to use to see her plans through."

Minthe frowns. "You think she was going to use Persephone?"

I don't think, I know. I simply do not know what she intended to use her for. "Yes, I do."

"But—" Minthe shakes her head. "Do you think she still wants to use her?"

Demeter has been searching for centuries for Persephone, just as I have. But she was not bound to the same restrictions she had the Moirai—the Fates—bind me. I've always thought it was because she wanted a second chance to poison her daughter against me. To ensure that I wasn't able to keep her for my own.

Now...

"Yes. I do think Demeter has other plans for Persephone. Plans for her ancient, abused soul."

"Persephone does not know she is a Goddess," Minthe speaks what I already know. Only confirming how truly dangerous, how viciously cruel Demeter really is.

Her core is rotten. The Goddess of harvest and agriculture is rotten, her core poisoned by her greed. And it makes sense now, the crops of the world dying as people reject whole nutrients for the rotten, poisoned foods assembled by corporations. The wheat that is stripped of nutrients and infused with toxins, preservatives. Demeter, the Goddess meant to feed the world, has been poisoned by the very greed she spills into the bellies of the needy, sparking a craving for more even in the knowledge that it will, eventually, kill them.

Rage is an ever-burning inferno in my gut as I think of my sister.

"Persephone will remember," I say confidently, though I do not know how I know. "In time, she will remember. Until then, we must work to reveal what it is Demeter planned to use her for. And if she plans to use her still."

CHAPTER
EIGHTEEN

P*ersephone*

THINGS HAVE FELT different between me and Hades since the night in the pool. Maybe that thing he stirred in me when we first met has fully awoken. Maybe it was just my time. Maybe it's the sun.

All I know is that my flesh feels alive. The blood in my veins stirs restlessly and the hum of need in my core is endless. I feel itchy in my skin with a need I am unable to scratch.

"How is work?" Hades asks from where he sips his coffee as I whip the eggs for an omelet. I no longer have to hurry quite so much in the mornings, since Hades now has a car take me directly to work. The man is spending far too much money on his need for a companion and cook.

"Hot." I smirk at him. "But good. We got a new girl. You won't believe her name."

He raises a brow in question. "I won't?"

"Minthe." I chuckle. "I feel like the Underworld has literally crept to the surface to meet me. Did you know, since I've been here, I've met a Hades, a Leuce, and now a Minthe?" I laugh incredulously. "I mean, what are the odds?"

Hades simply watches me the way he so often does. Like he can't look away.

My skin hums. My blood stirs.

I whip the eggs harder.

"Very few people even know who those—" he pauses, then murmurs, "*Characters* are."

I give him a dubious expression. "I'm pretty sure everyone knows who Hades is, Hades."

"Hades, perhaps." His smile is devilish. "But Minthe? And even less expected, Leuce?"

I shrug, conceding. "Minthe's story is very known. Leuce, though, I'll give you that. Her story is a bit less popular when it comes to the telling's of Underworld lore."

"But you are familiar with it? The myths of the Underworld, that is?"

Pouring the eggs into the buttered pan, I nod. "I love Greek lore. It's been a passion of mine since grade six when we did a unit on Ancient Greece."

"What about it do you find so intriguing?"

"Everything." I can't help but look at him, my heart skipping in its cage at the intensity I find in his dark eyes.

His lips curl. "And who is your favorite God?"

I roll my lips, narrowing my gaze on him. "I don't know why, but that feels like an awfully personal question."

He grins, but his voice is deep. Husky, even. "How so?"

I shrug, biting into my bottom lip and instantly regretting it for the way fire erupts in his eyes, igniting my core in the same. I look away, busying myself with adding veggies to the eggs, topping with cheese. I flip the omelet before covering it and letting it simmer to finish.

"I don't know. It just feels a little exposing."

"Will you expose yourself to me, then, Persephone?" The way he asks makes me feel like he's asking for more than to simply hear the name of my favorite God. Like he's asking me to strip right here in his kitchen, to bare my flesh to the devil in his eyes. To let him feast on the yearning he sparks alive inside me.

There is a low hunger in the depths of his voice that will not be sated by the omelet I'm cooking.

I shiver, blaming it on the air conditioning.

Suddenly, it seems less harmful to tell him my favorite God. "I've always been fascinated by Hades more than the rest."

"Is that so?"

Is that pleasure that hums in the deep of his voice?
"Yeah."

"What about the God of the Underworld fascinates you so much?"

I shrug again, wetting my lips. I feel oddly incapable of catching my breath. "I don't know."

It's a lie. I know exactly why the God of the Underworld fascinates me. But I can't tell him. *I can't.*

I hear his stool slide over obsidian tile as I avoid his gaze, sliding the omelet off the burner. I sense he's close when the air conditioning stops working, and heat erupts over every inch of my flesh. I don't understand how his mere presence burns me like an inferno when so many others avoid getting close to him. I've seen it more than once; the wide berth people give him. As though touching him sparks fear and threat of eternal torture. Maybe that's why he's paying me to be his companion. Maybe my lack of self-preservation when it comes to this man has inspired his desire to be close to me.

He's at my back now and my heart is threatening to rip from the cage of my ribs. It's beating so violently inside my chest; I imagine he can hear it. Breath tumbles from my lungs in tiny, sharp pants. As my hands grip the counter for purchase, they tremble.

I don't know what it is about Hades that sets me off like this. What is it about his nearness that rattles me this way?

"Are you afraid of me, Persephone?" God, he's so close. I can feel the hot wash of his breath against the shoulder my tank top has left bare.

"N-no." The word falls from little more than a breath into a space that crackles with electricity.

"I can practically hear the thunder of your heart." He isn't touching me, but the heat of his body touches every inch of my back. A caress of flame and sinful darkness that I desperately ache to sink into.

"I'm not afraid."

"Mmm." The low rumble carves the way for fire to spread in my veins. He observes, "You're trembling."

Breath rattles in my lungs. "I'm nervous."

"Why?" He's so close. He could touch me. He could kiss me.

God, but I want him to kiss me. I want him to taste me and ravish me and keep me...

As though he can hear my thoughts, he curses low. It's an agonized, hardly restrained thing of nearly broken need that strikes a lash of violent hunger deep within me.

I swallow the moan that threatens to break free, admitting instead, "Because I feel the need to tell you things I've never told anyone else. Things I wouldn't dare tell another soul."

"Like?"

I laugh. It's an incredulous sound. "I told you I was crazy within minutes of meeting you, Hades. I told you I hear a voice in my head."

"Mmm," he murmurs again. "And what do you feel the urge to tell me now, Persephone?"

"I—" I shake my head. "I can't. You won't look at me the same."

"The way I look at you could never change."

I scoff. "Yes, it could. I assure you."

His hands move to grip the counter, bracketing my body. He's still not touching me, but there is an air of dominance in this simple act that I've sensed from the man from the moment I met him. A dominance I've been unable to ignore.

Nerves erupt in my belly. I gasp a sharp inhale, the shards of it splintering in my lungs. Maybe it's this dominance that had me agreeing to the insanity of becoming his companion. Maybe it's the darkness I sense deep within him that calls to the cavernous pits of my hollow soul, where the echoing agony of a man I don't know has called for me all my life.

Maybe I really am crazy, hovering between reality and something fantastical that will send me into a spiral of insanity from which I will never recover.

His voice is deliciously rough, the only thing to touch me even though we stand so close, as he commands, "Tell me."

There is something in his command that has my lips parting, threatening to spill a truth I can't hide. My control has slipped, fractured by the magnitude of his power as the weight of his demand caresses me like I wish his touch would.

No, no. He is my boss. And he's so much older than me.

We wouldn't work. We wouldn't fit.

We're from two different times. He's lived life, while I've only just begun.

He urges, "Persephone."

I shudder. "It's his romance with Persephone. The way he took her, stole her." I think his breath catches. His fingers curl into the counter. *I can hardly breathe at all.* "It's wrong, Hades. I shouldn't—I know it's wrong. But I've always been so fascinated with his obsession of her, and how it drove him to claim her—even against her will. How he refused to let her go, manipulating and scheming in order to keep her for his own. I—"

The heat of his big body warms the space between us. The rumble of his deep voice strokes me like a physical touch. I am helpless to refuse when he urges, "Go on."

Quieter, I admit, "I wonder about the way he made her fall for him. How he managed to possess her heart after stealing her body." My breath hitches, my body aching with sharp desire that spills wet need into my panties in response to his big body hovering over mine. "I've always fantasized about having that for myself. Finding a man who claims me, all of me. Who steals my choice and forces my love. Who invades my heart with the same force he invades my body, as I imagine Hades did with Persephone. I—" I shake my head and shutter my eyes as fire spills into my cheeks. "I think—I think I'm more than crazy, Hades. I think I'm sick."

"I think you remember."

"Wh—" My words falter as he pushes away. I am assaulted by the cold of the AC, my body mourning his heat. His closeness.

I'm little more than a wobbly stand of Jell-O, struck by the way he moves, as though entirely unaffected, to pull two plates from the cupboard. He serves the omelet I cooked, and somehow, we eat as though nothing happened at all.

But before I leave to meet my ride, Hades catches me around the neck to pull me close. He brushes lips seared in flame across my brow. "You are not crazy, Persephone."

I don't know why, but as I step into the elevator, my ravaged soul weeps and hot tears spill.

I've never been more confused in all my life.

More aroused.

More *lost*.

CHAPTER
NINETEEN

P*ersephone*

THE SUN IS high in a cloudless, blue sky. Sweat coats my skin, dripping down my spine. I fear my blood is a degree from boiling. Every grain of sand that touches my oversensitive skin feels as though it's electrically charged.

I'm hot, but I have a feeling it's not entirely the fault of the sun.

I've been bothered since this morning with Hades.

Even though it's been hours, I've been unable to shake the aching need within me. The cord of want he struck has been humming deep all day, setting me on a frequency of annoyed arousal that I've never before played.

I want it to stop. I want to make it stop. To respond to it with what it wants. What it needs.

I'm in a mood because of it, and Addison's relentless flirting is only making things worse. I'm not used to men flirting with me, or really showing me any attention at all.

Back at home, I was the weird girl who, for the most part, failed to make friends. I was always a loner in school, focused more on my studies than I was on making friends. I attended church, and was polite to those who spoke to me, but the conversations I did have were mostly tag-along conversations my parents had already begun.

I was always just *there*.

I'm beginning to see that I was never really present. Behind my parents, I was simply the shadow. The extension of them.

But here in Greece, I stand on my own. I'm forging friendships, nurturing relationships, and learning the intoxicating blend of what it means to be a desirable young woman who has needs and wants of her own.

I am awakening.

Or that's what it feels like. I feel like I've lived my whole life without ever really experiencing anything. Maybe it was because I'd never really been free to experience.

Now, Mom and Dad aren't here to stop me. I

haven't been hearing the voice, either in sleep or awake to deter me. Finally, for the first time in my life, I feel as though I'm a girl like all the others.

"Persephone," Beth calls from where she works under the big white tent. Even with the distance between us, I can see the sheen of sweat on her tan skin. She waves me over. "Come here. Addison, too."

"What do you think we did?" Addison asks low.

I look at him, and he chuckles at my frown. "Nothing."

He drops his pitch to a whisper. "I think we're in trouble."

"For what?"

"Maybe we'll get detention together."

I scoff. "As if."

"Or maybe it's just you who is in trouble. You're hardly ever at the house. Always seeing to the needs of the rich dude at his. And you were almost late this morning." Something like fear spikes inside me. I was almost late. For some reason traffic had been bumper to bumper. Probably because it's been an off day, and an off day always ends up being the one where all the stuff goes wrong.

"I have a job, Addison. Some of us don't have rich parents that can support our every whim," I snap. "And if I'm in trouble, what did *you* do to be in trouble with me?"

Okay, I'm prickly. The heat must be getting to me.

Addison leans close. "I can be bad, Annie."

I roll my eyes. "I'll bet."

"I can show you." He slides closer. My skin heats when he challenges, "Just say the word."

From not too far away, Minthe's chime-like laughter sounds. "She's not into you, Addison."

I blink and give my head a confused little shake because *what the hell?* I pack up my tools and crush Addison just a little when I say, "I'm good."

I don't look back as I move from where I'd been dusting the base of what we suspect was another temple, now in ruins. Under the white tent, ancient artifacts we've unburied lay on clean white linen covered tables.

Beth smiles, her eyes drifting over my shoulder where I sense Addison is now standing close. "You guys need a break from the heat." She points to one of the tables. "You can start cleaning there. Of course, be careful."

"These hands know how to be gentle, Beth." I don't know how Addison can make everything sound so sexual. Most of it should be cringe, but everyone—literally everyone swoons.

Even now, the red in Beth's already heat-stained cheeks deepens. She giggles. "I have no doubt." Her eyes get big as they land on me and she breathes, "Have fun."

I smile, though it's a bit forced. Pulling my hat off, I fan my face as I take a seat at the table. Addison sits across from me and I can feel the way his bright blue eyes roam my face as we settle in to cleaning centuries old debris from the ancient artifacts.

"It doesn't work on you, does it?"

I lift my gaze to meet his. "What?"

"Flirting."

My lips part. Something in my belly flutters when his eyes chase my tongue as I wet them. Nervously, I shake my head. "Not really."

"Why not?"

I shrug, feeling awkward. "I think I might miss some of it."

He frowns. "What?"

"It just goes over my head a lot of the time." I peek at him and explain, "The flirting, I mean."

He sits back in his chair, studying me. "How so?"

"I've never been the girl guys flirted with. So now that it happens, I guess I just—it's just not something I expect."

"You've never been the girl guys flirt with?" His brows are arched high, like he doesn't believe me.

I don't know why he wouldn't. "That's what I said."

"How is that possible?"

I shift in my chair. There is a bubble of annoyance swelling inside me, because now I think he's playing with me. I don't like to be played with.

I sigh, lowering my tools to the table. "Addison," I start, but shake my head. He's watching me curiously, waiting attentively. I don't understand the game he's playing. "Do I feel like an easy mark to you?"

He looks taken aback. His chuckle is nervous, touched by wariness. "What? No."

"I am genuinely confused how I can go from living my whole life without a single boy being interested in me only to come here and be surrounded by men who—who—"

"Who what?"

"Who—" God, my face is burning. I feel hotter than I did under the sear of the sun. "*Argh*. I don't know, Addison. I don't know what you want from me."

He says nothing for a solid moment. He simply watches me, studying me with those intense blue eyes. He really is handsome. I can see why Claire thinks he's the hot one. There's an intensity to Addison that feels massive and ancient, like he's played this role a thousand times and honed it to perfection.

It's a crazy thought, but apparently, I'm full of them.

He finally speaks. "The guys in your hometown are stupid. That or they're blind."

Or they know I'm crazy and they're smart enough to stay far, far away.

My phone rings, saving me. At least, that's what I think until I see the name. With a sigh, I swipe to answer. Mom's smiling face fills the screen, and with years of practice, I replicate it. "Hey, Mom."

"Annie! Finally. You haven't been answering your phone at night."

Addison raises a brow, settling in to eavesdrop on my conversation. "I told you I got a job."

"Yes, but you don't work *all* night." Mom gives a condescending laugh. It's the one that's supposed to make me feel guilty. The one designed to make me do what she wants. Say what she wants. *Be* what she wants.

I don't know why it's not working now. It's always worked before.

Reigning in my annoyance, I explain, "I'm tired when I finally get to bed."

"Too tired to call home?"

"Actually, yeah." Mom blinks. There's a moment of alarm before her face smooths and she laughs again. "Oh, Annie. If your father can work all day in the fields and still make time to talk to you, I think you can play in the sand, cook a few meals, and do the same for him. Don't you?"

Addison huffs across the table and my eyes flit to him. He looks annoyed. His jaw grinds, but he remains silent.

I hide my frown behind a smile. "Sure, Mom. I'll try harder."

"Good. Then we'll talk tonight, with your father." Mom grins her megawatt grin. It's the one that says she knows she's won.

She always wins, though. In every area of her life, against every opponent.

"Sure."

"How is the cooking job going?"

"Good." I told her I was cooking. She thinks I'm in a restaurant. I haven't corrected her. "I like it."

"You've always enjoyed cooking."

"How's the farm?"

"It's hard here, Annie. It's the worst year we've had since as far back as I can remember."

I hum. "Must be the heat."

"And the lack of rain." She frowns. "Your father thinks you're a lucky charm. I'm inclined to agree. Everything grows better with you around."

"Mom." I just keep from rolling my eyes. Just. "I'm not a charm."

"I'm serious, Annie. Even the flowers in the shop have noticed your absence." She pushes her hair over her shoulder. "It'll be nice when you come home where you belong."

I don't belong there. "I miss you too, Mom."

"You know," Mom starts. "I was talking with Pastor Tanner—" Mom leans in to the phone as she would if I were home for the gossip. "And he said they're very lax about the age of intoxication there in Greece. Is that true?"

"I'm not sure what you're asking me."

"Have you been in those clubs, Annie?" Her eyes narrow. "Have you been consuming the alcohol?"

Across the table, Addison chokes on a laugh. I let my eyes drift heavenward before looking back at my waiting mother. "No, Mom. I haven't."

"That's good. Very good. Because you know what they say about that kind of girl. The girl that drinks and entertains boys." Mom lowers her voice, but not low enough. "They're loose and used. I don't know why I let your father make me worry, though. We raised you to know right and wrong, to keep your legs closed and your sensibilities intact. You're not a whor—"

"Mom!" I can't even make myself look at Addison.

"I'm just saying. You know you have a nice church boy waiting here for you when you come home."

"There's no one waiting there for me."

"Nonsense! Mrs. Opal's grandson—"

"Annie." Mom is cut off by Addison's deep, firm voice calling my name. "Personal calls are for personal time."

Mom looks like she's about to give Addison a piece of her mind, but I hurry to say, "Sorry. Gotta go, Mom. Love you."

I don't wait for her reply before I disconnect. I drop my head into my hands and groan. "I'm sorry."

"Don't be."

"That was awful."

"Yeah, it was," Addison agrees soberly.

"Thanks for saving me."

"Sounded like you needed saving." I've never heard

Addison talk without that playful lilt. Even when he's goofing around with Theo, that boyish charm is there in his voice, his eyes, the movements of his body. He's charm personified, but right now, he's—well, I think he's angry.

"Sorry," I say again.

He rolls his lips. "Does she always talk to you like that?"

I wet my own lips, nodding slowly. Hesitantly. "I think so."

"What do you mean, you think so?"

I wince. "Mom has always been—she's always been *her*. I don't think I really realized it though because I was always there. Always living it. She loves me. I know she loves me. But she's—well, she's opinionated."

"She's a manipulative narcissist." His brows rise and fall like he's surprised by his own words. He mutters under his breath, "That's saying it nicely."

I twist my lips to the side. "Maybe."

"She is, Annie. I'm telling you; she is."

I shrug a helpless shrug. "She's my mother."

CHAPTER
TWENTY

P*ersephone*

WHEN I ARRIVE at the penthouse to the scent of fresh herbs, something coiled inside me relaxes. It's been a long day, and I'm beyond exhausted. The thought of cooking left me feeling tense and overwhelmed, so I'm happy I won't have to. Still, I can't help the guilt I feel at the thought that I'll be shucking my responsibilities for the evening. Responsibilities Hades is paying me to see to.

Bending to give the eagerly waiting pups some scratches, I speak low, "Hey guys. You know this isn't permanent. I'm only here for a few months." Noc gives a low whine, as though he understands what I'm saying, and doesn't like it. "You're worming your way into my heart. It's really going to hurt when I have to leave."

Jas bumps her head into my palm. There's something aware in the deep of her beautiful golden eyes. I drop to my knees when she scoots closer, her chest bumping mine as though to ask me to put my arms around her. I do, without hesitation.

Against her sleek black fur, I whisper, "I'm falling for you all so hard and fast."

I tell myself I'm not including the man in that as I squeeze Jas tighter. I'm lying.

Prim gives a low growl, and I pull away to give her a stroke. "Urgh." I give myself a shake as I sniffle back emotion I can't begin to understand. "It must be my time of the month. I'm beyond emotional right now."

Or it was just a *really* long day.

Prim blinks knowingly at me—even though I know she *can't* know. She's a dog, after all. Still, I shudder at the weight of Noc's midnight blue gaze as he watches over us all. Off-balance and clearly overly hormonal, I lose my balance as I attempt to stand and fall on my butt. As my luck would have it, that's the moment Hades appears.

The difference between the two of us is glaringly obvious. For once, it has nothing to do with the fact he has his life together while I haven't even figured out a sure career path. It has nothing to do with the gap in our ages, or even the wealth he holds that I can't begin to comprehend, nor will I ever attain even a fraction of his worth.

The glaring difference is in the way he holds himself. Where I am insecure and uncertain, he is confident and sure. Where I am chaos, he is order. Where I am soft, he is incredibly firm. I'm a sticky mess of sweat and hormones in a pile of emotions on his floor, and he is the pinnacle of composure in fitted black slacks with a black button-down shirt tucked in and split by a black leather belt. The first few buttons are undone to expose the toned skin of a hard, golden chest.

The way his long legs are spread, his big hands dipped lazily in the pockets of his slacks, his square jaw hard and his black eyes pinned firmly on me—he is pure power. It radiates off him like heat radiates off the sun. He could burn me if he wanted, I'm sure of it.

Hades says nothing as he leans a shoulder into the wall, settling in to watch me on the floor with his dogs. I give Prim another stroke and share a blushing look with Noc before I gather the gumption to find my feet. I feel sticky from the long day. Gross in comparison to the obvious glamor that clings to the man.

"Hey," I finally muster a greeting. I get a small chin lift in response. His quiet sets nerves flying inside my chest. "Um—did you cook?"

"Ordered in."

"Why?"

"I wanted to."

"But you hired me to cook for you. That's why I'm here."

His eyes drag over my body slowly. His broad chest expands with a deep breath before he releases it slowly. "I wanted a slow evening, Persephone. It looks like you could also use a night off."

"That bad, eh?"

His lips twitch. "Canadians really do say that?"

"Hmm?" I'm confused.

"Eh."

My already warm cheeks warm more. "Oh, that. Yeah. We do."

"Cute."

"We can't help it." He smiles a soft, barely there smile in response. When he says nothing else, I murmur, "Since I'm not cooking, would it be okay if I took a shower before I join you? It was hotter than Hell out today and I'm beat."

"Hades."

"What?" I ask at his bizarre reply.

"Hotter than Hades, Persephone. Even more accurately, hotter than Tartarus. Hell doesn't exist."

"Wait, you actually believe that?" I can't tell if he's joking with me or not.

"Believe what?"

"That Hell doesn't exist."

"It doesn't. At least not in the way you're thinking of it."

I feel my jaw unhinge. "You still believe in the old Gods?"

"Of course."

"No one believes in them. Hades—" I can't help the little shiver that pulses through my body. I follow up the discomfort with a little laugh, if only to ease the spill of ice I feel overtaking my veins. "The ancient Gods are myth."

His lips thin. His voice is impossibly quiet and impossibly dark. "If you say so, Persephone."

I find it hard to believe that such an intelligent man can believe that the Gods of old are real. That the excuses the people made to explain the ways of life and the world to themselves, that ancient fabrications of a creative mind, is real.

For a moment, we simply stare at each other. My mind is stacking reasons to tell him why the Gods aren't real. To *prove* that they aren't real.

I've wanted my whole life for the ancient Gods of myth to be real. I've dreamed of them as though they were real. I've fantasized about them and felt the spark of fear inside my chest at the idea that they could possibly be real. And yet faced with another who believes in them wholly, I can do nothing but deny the existence of beings I've always hoped *could* be true.

Instead of voicing all the reasons the man before me is even crazier than I am, I say softly, "I'm going to shower."

Hades simply gives me another chin lift, but he

doesn't move from the wall as I pass him with his three dogs in tow.

I FEEL LESS OF A MESS, and definitely less sticky when I meet Hades in the kitchen again. He is sitting at the end of the long kitchen table with a sleek black laptop and a glass of deep red wine. He finishes whatever it is he's typing when he sees me, closing the laptop.

I expect him to rise from his chair to join me, but he doesn't. He sits back, lifts his wine from the table, and pins his dark gaze to me.

I stand my ground, refusing to fidget under his inspection even though I want to. As his eyes roam over my body, drinking in every inch of me, I feel far less dressed than I am. In workout shorts and an oversized, loose white t-shirt, I'm not inappropriately dressed. But the way he looks at me makes me feel like I am.

"Feel better?" he finally asks. His voice is rough, like he's been drinking whiskey instead of wine.

I nod, but have to swallow to clear the lump in my throat before I'm able to stammer, "Um, yeah."

"Good." He rises from the table and moves into the kitchen where he pulls two plates from the oven, sliding them over the counter. He winks. "Dinner is served."

My heart flips. I slide onto a stool. "Thanks."

Hades pours me a glass of the wine he's drinking, then he rounds the island to sit adjacent to me. Woodsmoke and man surround me, infused with enough danger to make my head woozy. I lift my wine, foolishly attempting to clear the dizzying effect of the man with alcohol.

"What made today so hard?" Hades asks after a few bites.

I frown. "How do you know today was hard?"

His lips twitch. God, but the man is so freaking handsome. It's not fair how handsome he is. It's not fair how he is aware of how handsome I think he is. I'm too young to have a man like him. To want a man like him. Obviously, my body hasn't figured that out because it's *not* on the same page as my brain.

"You were sprawled on my entryway floor moments from sobbing your woes to my dogs, Persephone. I'd say your day was rough."

Fire flares in my cheeks, reflecting in the deep of his eyes. I drop my own to my plate. "It was hot today."

"That can't be the reason."

"Why not? Lots of people struggle in the heat."

"Not you." His eyes drift hungrily over me. "You're built for heat, aren't you, Persephone?"

Oh wow. I swallow. Hard.

I change the subject. "I spoke with my mom today."

He's quiet for a beat. All the teasing washes from his eyes. "Tell me about it."

I pull in breath that rattles inside the cage of my chest. "She can be difficult. Today was one of the times where she was."

"How so?"

"She's just—she's judgy, I guess." I sigh, pushing potatoes around my plate. "The worst part was Addison," I pause to explain. "One of the guys I work with, well, he heard it all. And then he saved me from her."

Hades tenses. It's faint, but it's there. "How did he save you?"

"I was paired with him today. Normally, he's flirty and easygoing. Today, during the call, I saw a different side of him. He gave me an excuse to hang up on her that I wouldn't have to pay for later. But after the call, he stayed serious. He was someone I could actually talk to, you know? Just different from his usual. Still, I had a hard time feeling like myself after that call, and Addison respected that."

Hades studies me a moment too long. Discomfort blooms over my skin and I shift in my chair as I pick at my chicken.

"Is he someone you can see yourself with?" His voice is smooth, but there's an undercurrent of something dark and dangerous. A riptide that threatens to pull me under.

"You mean romantically?" Hades nods and I shake

my head. "I'm not sure. I don't have a lot of romantic experience."

He raises a brow. "No?"

I blush. "No."

"Are you attracted to him?"

I'm attracted to you. "He's handsome." *I shouldn't be attracted to you.* "And age appropriate."

I can't believe I said that. What the hell is wrong with me?

Hades' grin is ruggedly delicious. "Age appropriate?"

I slide off the stool. "Dinner was delicious, Hades, but I can't eat another bite. Thank you."

He sips his wine and watches as I clear my plate into a container for lunch tomorrow. By the time I'm finished, his plate is cleared so I busy myself with loading the dishwasher, happy to do something to earn my pay.

When I turn around, I see that Hades has refilled my wine glass, and is already walking into the living room. Swiping my glass from the counter, I follow him. I take a seat on the massive sectional, careful to put space between us.

I've been losing the plot lately when it comes to Hades. After the night in the pool, and then this morning—space is smart.

I need space.

Without space, I'm liable to do something stupid.

"Tell me about Addison," Hades says after a moment.

I frown. I'm surprised he's still thinking about Addison. "Um, I don't know what to say."

"You think he is attractive."

"Well, I mean, I think every girl thinks he's attractive." I blush a bright shade of cherry red and sip my wine in another foolish attempt to cool down. It does nothing but heat my blood. "He's kind of an Adonis."

Hades makes a noise of surprise, for the first time since I've known him, losing his composure. "What did you say?"

"You know the expression. A player. A man all the women swoon for."

He clears his throat. "Do you swoon for him?"

I consider. "Not really, no."

I'm kind of stupidly obsessed with fantasizing about my very unattainable boss.

"But?"

I don't know how the man always knows when there's more. He can read me like no other. Not even my parents, who have known me since my very first breath, know me like Hades seems to know me. It's disconcerting and yet not. Under all the bewildering *how's*, there's a comfort in being so easily read by someone else.

"I'm going to be twenty years old, Hades, and I've never been kissed." *Okay, I don't know why I tell him that.*

Must be that weird ability the man has to pull every truth, uncomfortable or otherwise, from the deep of me. I shift, unnerved. "I've never had a boyfriend or experimented or—" I loose a shaky sigh, pushing a lock of hair behind my ear as I resettle myself on the couch. "It feels nice to have someone want me, I guess. To be interested in me." I can't believe I'm saying this. "And I think I'm just a little curious."

"Curious about what?" His voice is rough and husky. A little breathless.

It affects me. Intimately. "What it might feel like to be with someone."

His eyes heat, but he doesn't reply. At least not right away. Instead, he takes a long sip of his wine. "I see."

He takes another deep drink. I watch as his throat bobs, shocked by the thought that drifts through my mind. I want to crawl across the couch toward him. I want to taste his skin. Want to feel his throat bob under my tongue.

What the actual hell?

The sun is getting to me. It has to be.

There is no other explanation. Never in my life have I felt this way. Never have I had thoughts such as the ones I've been entertaining about Hades.

My body feels tingly and sensitive.

I stand abruptly. The pups stand from their beds, alert. Noc's eyes shift between me and Hades and the door. He senses something about me is off. Smells it, I can tell.

A low sound leaves his chest and the girls both drop their heads.

Hades lifts a hand. A single hand, and all three drop their butts to the floor. Just like that.

My heart is slamming in my chest. I sense that the pups can hear it.

I need to escape.

Feeling silly and sensitive and a whole bunch of other emotions, I stumble over my words. "I should—I should um—go to bed."

TWENTY-ONE

 *ades*

HER SOUL SENSES the ancient history we share, even if her memories of me—of us—are tainted by the damning effects of her tragic murder, lost to the rapids of The Lethe.

Her body knows what her mind can't yet accept. That she is mine.

That she belongs with me.

The ancient God within me is growing restless as the days pass, bleeding into weeks. He is more than aware that she is close to him. The mate he's longed for, for centuries. He hungers for her, his desperation simmering under the flesh of the man. *Take her*, he whispers, *mark her, steal her.*

I drag my palms down my face, restless and irritable. I need more time with her. I hunger for her when she is gone from me. The pull of her is massive. The worry is relentless torture.

"You're losing it," Leuce tells me what I already know. "Maybe you should just tell her."

"I can't. Not yet."

She sits back in the couch, lifting an arm to drop it lazily against the back of the couch. "Why not?"

A low growl of irritation rumbles in my chest. "You know why."

"No, I don't, Hades."

"She doesn't love me." I glare across the room where my ex-lover and friend sits. "She is human, Leuce."

She scoffs. "She isn't."

"She smells human."

"But she isn't. She has the soul of a Goddess."

I feel my lip curl. "Her body is human. Vulnerable."

"Take her to the Underworld."

"It's not that simple."

She rolls her silver-green eyes. "You keep saying. What I don't understand is what's different this time around. You took her before, and she fell in love with you. She's already halfway there, Hades. I've seen the way she looks at you."

My blood heats at the thought of Persephone

looking at me with want. I've sensed it, too. The hunger that burns under her skin. The desire that swims in her veins, simmering in the marrow of her bones. But it's not enough.

"I need her heart."

"You'll get it. Eventually."

Tension spreads inside me like poison. I admit what I have yet to admit to anyone. The words fall quiet, but she hears them. "I need her soul."

The very breath in Leuce's chest stills. She is stiff, frozen for an entire minute. "Her *soul*?"

"It's the only way I can keep her safe. Can ensure that she will never be taken from me again."

"But you can't *take* a soul, Hades."

I grit my teeth. "I am aware, Leuce."

My patience is thinning. Such a thing is very, very dangerous.

"It must be given."

"I know."

"Freely."

Rage and something much worse—*fear*—bubble in my chest. Because it's not a simple or easy thing, to give a soul. It is not a thing done lightly, and the consequences are more than massive. They are eternal. And as such, they are consequences I'm not confident she will ever be *willing* to pay.

She has been raised in the Christian religion. Her idea of Hades has been greatly distorted by her view of the devil, a thing of evil. I am a much more complex God.

I am multifaceted, but the fact remains, considering I predate the devil and the formation of the Christian religion by well over a thousand years, like the formation of the Roman and Egyptian Gods, pieces of my puzzle have been plucked and molded to fit the narrative of a new God, or in the devil's case, a fallen angel. One such puzzle piece is the rare dealings I make with souls. Although butchered massively by Christianity's spin on the devil's determination to damn souls in earthly dealings, my dealings for souls are far more complex. Intricate, even. Still, the comparisons remain, and one aware of the devil's ways as Persephone is would be hard pressed to promise me her everlasting soul.

I sit back in my chair. Leuce's eyes track my fingertips as I rub them into my jaw. "Such is my dilemma."

Leuce bows her head for a moment, chin meeting her chest. She's thinking, her mind racing for another way.

She won't find one.

I've considered every angle, for centuries. The only way to ensure Persephone's eternal safety with me is to possess her eternal soul.

Anxiety spikes inside me. A feeling I am unaccustomed to, but have been plagued by since her return in my life.

I need more time with her.

I need to show her that she doesn't simply want me, but that she needs me.

I need her to crave me as I crave her.

I need her heart if I am ever to possess her soul.

But more time with her, time spent in the day, *in public*, could—*will* put her in danger.

"What are you going to do?" Leuce interrupts my scattered thoughts. She shifts on the couch, planting her elbows into her knees as she leans forward.

She, too, is agitated. Like I can smell the defence-less human that clings to Persephone's skin, I can smell the worry, spiked with fear, that wafts from Leuce's pores now.

I stand, straightening my shoulders. "Right now, I'm going to take her to lunch."

TWENTY-TWO

P*ersephone*

HADES WAS RIGHT when he said I like the heat. Even though the sun beats down on me, and I'm unbearably hot, I can't quite get enough of the bone-deep warmth that spills from the sun in the sky. When everyone else is hiding from the heat, I'm soaking it up.

I know better, I really do. Beth has called me in from the heat to hide under the big tents they've erected to protect us all from the rays. In the first weeks, I'd been happy to spend time under the shade of the tent—but now not so much.

I can't explain it, this deep hunger that swells like an ache inside me to sit out under the golden rays. I'm fair of skin with hair more white than blonde. I should fear the sun, the burns and cancer Mom warns of.

Yet I hunger for it. For the warmth.

I never noticed back home, covered in sunscreen and concealed under hats, how deeply the hunger for the warmth inside me ran. It's a balm for my soul. Nourishment I didn't know I needed.

Stripped of my mother's constant nagging to apply another coat of sunscreen, my father's warning to put my hat back on my head, I'm free to feel the world around me *for me*.

Shrugging the light shirt from my shoulders, I let the sun kiss my pale skin as I take a seat on a big stretch of warm stone. I stretch out my legs and pull my hair from the high ponytail, letting the strands fall to tickle the sweat-dewy skin left exposed by my tank top.

My head is tipped back, my face free of sunscreen to bask in the rays of liquid gold that pours from the sky when I hear a rustle of movement beside me. I nearly groan, thinking it's Addison come to flirt again like he has all morning, when I spot Minthe.

She's settled in beside me in much the same way I am. Legs stretched out; hands planted on the warm stone behind her so that she can lean back to catch the rays. As though we don't get pelted by the sun all day long, every day.

Like me, she's wearing shorts. Unlike me, deep green ink stretches up in a twist of vines from her feet, over her calves, to fade into the flesh of her thighs. Minthe is exotic and gorgeous in a way I can't ever hope to be. Her glossy, soil-colored hair is cut short, the sharp line of her bob just reaching her shoulders.

"Do you ever get enough of the sun?" She gives me a sideways look with shocking green eyes that spear me like thorns.

"Do you?"

Instead of answering, she throws her gaze to the white tent. I follow her gaze to where Addison sits, watching us. "The guy's soaked through his clothes, but he's still debating coming out here to flirt with you." She laughs, a chimelike sound with just a hint of tension. "Well, he was until I came over."

I've noticed that although Minthe likes most people, and is extremely friendly, she's a little less so around Addison.

I cast my gaze out over the land, a flicker of something warm spreading in my chest. It's the same something warm that I feel whenever I look out over this ancient earth. I feel, oddly, like my soul knows this place.

It's silly.

I'm crazy.

I sigh. "Addison likes to flirt. He's harmless."

"Is he?"

When I shoot a frown at Minthe, I find she's tipped her head back and closed her sharp green eyes. "What do you mean?"

"I think he has feelings for you." Her eyes are still closed. "Feelings are never harmless."

"I don't understand."

Minthe's chimelike laugh sounds again, this time with a hint of huskiness. She lifts her hand to run it through her hair and I'm slammed with a scent of mint so strong, and so familiar, I'm speechless. Memories that aren't mine assault me. Soft lips on mine, the taste of mint on my tongue. The touch of...

I stand abruptly as Minthe's eyes flutter open, her lips spreading into a smile that feels oddly knowing. "Is something wrong, Persephone?"

"Annie," I gasp. I can't seem to catch my breath. Or explain the sudden attraction I feel toward this woman —when I've never felt attraction to a woman before.

What in the world is happening to me?

Minthe stands, lifting a bottle of water to her lips. Through the sweat that clings to the cold bottle, I watch mint leaves dance in the water. Minthe smiles. "That's not your name."

"It's the name everyone calls me."

"Not everyone." She eyes me coyly, grinning the same.

I frown. "I don't know what you're talking about."

"Oh, come on now. I know you're working for Hades Pluton."

"Everyone knows that." *What is she getting at?*

"Breathe, Persephone. My girlfriend works for

Hades. I do, too, actually. As a waitress." She winks at me.

"Who is your girlfriend?" Even as I ask, I already suspect I know.

"Leuce."

Yep, I knew.

"I've met her," I admit. "She's intimidatingly gorgeous."

"She is." She sucks her bottom lip into her mouth, releasing it slowly. Another throb of unexpected attraction slams inside me, and I frown.

It's not *my* attraction, or at least I don't think it is. It feels distant, somehow. Impersonal.

And yet...

I'm confused. I don't know what this means?

Am I attracted to women?

I give my head a firm shake. "You said you know Hades?"

"Oh, yes. I do."

I frown. I feel as though I've stepped into some warped version of the Twilight Zone. "It's bizarre, isn't it?"

Minthe tips her head to the side. "What?"

"All of us meeting like this. Finding each other."

A slow smile spreads, but her brow knits. "What do you mean?"

"Our names. Minthe, Leuce, Hades, and Persephone. Isn't that a weird coincidence?"

She shrugs. "I suppose. Or maybe it just means we're supposed to know each other."

"Maybe." I hear myself agree, but I'm not sure. It feels like more, my connection to these people who share ancient names in this modern time.

And that's when I really know I'm losing the plot. Because I think we have any ties to the ancient, mythical beings who lived in a time well before my own.

Argh, maybe I should be sitting out of the sun like the rest of my team. There's a good chance Dad was right, and I've cooked my brain without my hat.

Oh well, I was already on board the crazy train. What's a little sun thrown onto the raging fire of insanity that is me?

"Hey," Minthe calls my attention back to her. "Me and a few friends are planning on going out this weekend. You should join us."

"I don't—" I start to tell her that I don't club, but something has the words dying on my tongue. "You know what? I'd love to."

Minthe's lips spread into a cat-like grin. It's sly. If I knew her better, I'd suspect she had something up her sleeve. But since I don't know her, I allow myself to suspect nothing.

All I can think is that I want to know her. *I need to know her.*

It's the same need I feel to know Hades.

CHAPTER

TWENTY-THREE

P *ersephone*

"SPEAK OF THE DEVIL," Minthe purrs over my shoulder, her eyes again on the tent. I twist to see a man I'd recognize in a crowd of millions.

My heart gives a single, hard throb, before it takes off my chest. The beat is racing at a pace I can't contain. I feel breathless and oversensitive as tingles of awareness spread over my body like fire in a dry forest. The heat that touches my skin suddenly feels a thousand times hotter than the sun. Wilder. More intimate. My craving for it far, far more than my hunger for the sun.

Hades is speaking with Beth under the white tent. I haven't had much chance to see him surrounded by others. Our time together has been mostly private, aside from that first night in the room filled with his art.

He towers over her. Over everyone.

The man stands at an impossible height, emanating a power that should intimidate me. It doesn't, though. Instead, I feel safe under the breadth of his immense power.

Beth, however, shifts uncertainly. But even still, there is a blush to her skin and a light to her eyes that tells me she's attracted to him. Every woman is attracted to Hades Pluton. But the glaring fact that Beth is beautiful and far closer to Hades' age than I am hits me like an icy wave. I'm drenched in a wash of jealousy that makes me feel icky and small.

Again, I wonder what is wrong with me.

But why is he here? Why is he talking to her?

Beth's hands are flying as she talks to Hades. I feel a little relief when I see the head of the program, Ralph, scurrying from the privacy of his tent. Ralph very rarely leaves his tent. His claim is that he's overwhelmed by paperwork, which is probably true.

He looks shaken by Hades' presence. Does everyone know who the man is here? Is he famous for the art he refuses to sell or for the nightclub everyone in Greece seems to know about?

Ralph clasps Hades' hand, giving it a firm shake. I can see his mouth moving fast, but I'm too far to know what they're talking about. It's clear they know each other, which is surprising. I wouldn't have expected Hades to know the awkward head of the archeology program, who is more comfortable pouring over paperwork than he is conversing with his team. The man takes introverted to a whole new level, which is just fine, because he has Beth to do all the extroverted things that need doing, and the girl is the definition of outgoing.

Still, Hades obviously knows Ralph.

I catch the scent of fresh mint, distracting me momentarily from Hades as Minthe says, "Wonder what he's doing here. Probably something to do with giving another donation."

"What?"

"He's the program's biggest sponsor."

I feel my head notch back in surprise. "He is?"

"Yeah." Minthe's hair shines in the sun as she nods. "He's the reason I got in late. I missed the deadline to enroll, but when I spoke to him about it, he said he could help me." She flashes straight white teeth with a wide smile. "And *voila*. He did."

I frown as I look back at Hades again. He knows this is where I spend my days. It's not like we haven't talked about where I go every day when I leave his home. I find it weird that he failed to mention he has a connection with the program. Obviously, it's a big connection if he can pull a string and get another student into the already full program.

I feel oddly duped.

I don't know why.

As though sensing that my thoughts have moved from jealousy and confusion to something darker, Hades' eyes shift to land on me. My heart jolts in my chest. It's as though he knew exactly where I was.

Had he spotted me before I'd spotted him?

Again, why is he here?

Hades says something and both Ralph and Beth look to me. I don't know why, but something inside me screams *run*. My inner voice warning me to flee.

I feel like the prey as his long strides devours the distance between us.

I don't know why I feel this way now. I've never felt unsafe with Hades. Never.

"Persephone," he says my name in his rough voice when he's close. Beside me, I swear I hear Minthe suck in a sharp breath. "Will you join me for lunch?"

"I—my break is almost finished."

His lips twitch. "I've cleared your absence."

I don't know how I feel about that. It's invasive and a little presumptuous—but still, I find myself nodding. The foolish fact is that I want to join him. I want to be with him.

Before I've thought it through, I hear myself agree quietly, "Okay."

"Good." Hades gives his attention to Minthe. "How are you liking things here?"

"Oh." There's a friendly lilt to her words that has my curiosity spiking. "I'm liking things just fine, Hades."

He smiles a soft, warm, familiar smile. My spiked curiosity red-lines. "That is good to hear, Minthe."

Questions whirl inside my mind as Hades touches his hand to my back, guiding me through the tent. I can't help but notice the way Addison's striking blue eyes are dark with something ugly as he watches me leave with Hades. Inside, I'm a storm of feelings.

As Hades guides me from the site to a flashy black sports car with a badge I don't have the expertise to place, I try to pick apart the threads of the storm that brews inside me. I try to decipher the mess of my feelings. I fail.

Hades closes the door and rounds to the other side. Even with his massive bulk, he moves fluidly into the seat next to me. The scent of woodsmoke and sinful thoughts swirls a ribbon of temptation around me. My body responds like it always responds to his nearness. To the scent of him. With an aching need I can't contain or control.

"Have you eaten already?" I shake my head in answer. Hades slips a pair of shades over his eyes. "Are you hungry?"

I'm starving. My body is ravenous.

I breathe, "Yes."

Through the reflective tint of his sunglasses, I feel his eyes on me. Behind his beard, a muscle in his jaw throbs. I swallow hard and force my gaze out the window.

Hades puts the car into gear and butterflies erupt in my belly as he takes off.

TWENTY-FOUR

P*ersephone*

"Why didn't you tell me you were involved in the archeology program?" Popping a garlic and herb seasoned shrimp into my mouth, I wait for his reply.

"I didn't think it mattered."

"Why didn't you tell me you knew Minthe?" I press. "I mentioned her to you when she started. I know I did."

I would have mentioned anyone with her name.

His dark eyes connect with mine and he rolls his lips. "Minthe is a friend of mine. A good friend. I wanted you to know her on your own before you became aware of my relationship with her."

I tense. "What is your relationship with her?"

His mouth twitches. "I just told you. She is a very good friend."

I frown, sitting back in my chair. "Why does it feel like you know so much more about me than I know about you, Hades?"

"Because I prefer to talk about you, Persephone."

I hate that his words set off fireworks inside me. I hate that I love the sound of his rough voice, and ache in the dark of the night to know what it would feel like to have his voice whispering, rough and hungry across my naked flesh.

Alarmed, I sit up straight in my seat. I shake the vision from my mind and wish I could shake the sting of red that tints my skin in the same way. I can't.

"You're blushing," Hades notes.

"Am I?" I play daft, nibbling on another shrimp.

"You are." He studies me. It only makes me hotter. "Why?"

"No reason."

"There's always a reason."

I challenge his gaze with my own. "Maybe I don't want to tell you."

"Why?"

I nibble the corner of my lip. "Maybe it's private."

"Well, now my interest is piqued. You have to share."

I feel breathless. "I don't."

Hades leans into the table, the scent of him

180

invading my space like I wish he would invade my body. God, what is wrong with me? When did I become so—sex-crazed?

And what is it about this man that makes me want to offer every inch of myself to him? What is it about him that makes me long to shatter my innocence?

"Persephone." *God, the way he says my name.* With the hint of threat wrapped up in decadent warning dipped in a delicious dare.

I shift in my seat, desperate to relieve the pressure I feel between my legs.

Hades' nostrils flare.

My heart thunders.

I swear, I see fire in his eyes.

Forgetting the bustling restaurant around us, I decide to enter this game he wants me to play. I take him up on his dare. But first, I lift my water to my lips, swallowing deep and licking the cool drops from the edge of the glass. Hunger flares in his eyes.

I'm playing with fire.

The man is far more experienced than me in the art of seduction.

But I want this. Him. Us. Shattered innocence and that rough whisper against the soft of my skin.

What if I did this with him? What if I gave him me these next months?

It wouldn't have to mean anything more than what it is. I'd be sure to keep my heart firmly in check. Under lockdown. But I'm going to be twenty next spring. I'm nineteen now, a woman. Young, yes. But a woman all the same.

I know what I want. This isn't a conclusion I've come to quickly. It's been a build-up of need and desire for weeks. This is not impulse. I've dreamed of him. Fantasized and hungered. I've worked through the guilt of it, the improperness and the disappointment my parents would feel knowing I had been with a man so much older.

So, they don't have to know.

I can do this with Hades. Have a summer fling. I can explore myself as I explore him. And then I can return to my life back home in Alberta.

What's the worst that could happen if I do this crazy thing and try my hand at tempting Hades? He could reject me, of course. But I don't think he will.

"Persephone," he presses when I give him nothing. I think I hear hunger in his voice, swear I see fire flickering in his eyes before it's gone. "Tell me."

I lean into the table, pushing my hair back as he drags his gaze over me. "You want to know what I was thinking? What made me blush?"

"Yes."

"I was thinking of what it might feel like..." I pause, wetting my lips. He's an artist, and I want to paint a picture for him. "I wonder what it would be like to feel your rough voice whispering across my naked body, painted in moonlight. To feel your touch burning into my skin, the mark of your kiss. I want to know; would you devour my sighs as you stole my innocence? Would you swallow them with your kisses? Or would you let the melody of them soar to mingle with the groans of pleasure you'd gift me?" He looks struck. A predator locked in a dance with his prey. I am hunted, and God, but I want him to devour me. Boldened by the hunger that flares in his gaze, I continue, "I wonder, Hades, what it would be like to be yours, if only for a night."

Darkness bursts from the depths of him. A thing I'm not sure I should have tempted. But it's too late now.

Excitement mingles with the trepidation as I shift in my seat. There is a part of me—the smarter part— that urges me to flee. I don't. I stand my ground, heart pounding, desire building.

His voice is a lash of longing across my ravenous heart. A hunger yawns inside me deeper than the pits of hell and more vast than Heaven.

"It would never be just one night."

TWENTY-FIVE

P*ersephone*

I THOUGHT Hades was going to steal me away to his condo on the top of the tower after the little picture I painted him, taunting him as I did. Instead, after I'd protested vehemently and rather loudly, he'd returned me reluctantly to the dig site with an ominous warning that has played on repeat in my mind since.

"It would feel better than you could ever imagine, my voice against your naked skin. I would spill your moans and devour your sighs. I would bleed myself into the marrow of your bones, and invade your very soul. I would steal your innocence, covet it. Treasure it always. I would make you mine, Persephone. Wholly and completely. Be ready for me."

I'd been unable to think the rest of the day. I've drifted back and forth between excitement for what is to come and fear for the fact I've tempted a man obviously more experienced than me. What I don't feel is regret.

Because even as I am afraid, I can't stop thinking that this is everything that I never knew I needed. And it hasn't escaped me that I haven't heard that anguished cry of my name since I came here. Since the night I met Hades.

There is a part of me, a silly, childish part that believes in the fantastical just enough to entertain the idea that maybe, just maybe that cry was my souls desperate need to find his. Or his to find mine. That silly part of me basks in the fantasy that maybe I was always meant to find Hades. Always intended for him. To be his.

I know it's crazy. Ludicrous. But I've always believed in soul mates, even though I never felt confident I would find mine.

And Hades can't be mine, either. Can he?

He's so much older than me. More experienced. More wealthy. More *everything*.

What can I possibly have to offer him other than my youth? What do I have to offer a relationship with a man who has everything? The whole world at his fingertips?

I've never felt so lacking.

I'd denied the car Hades sent for me to walk instead. I'd felt the need for the sun, to work off some of the agitation I felt coiling inside my body, tightening my nerves into springs a moment from snapping. I still don't feel regret, even as I'm helpless to slip inside my head.

I'm unsure of what I started. What it really means —the structure of what we will become now.

I don't know what I'm going to do now that I've opened a door I'm not sure I can close. I'm not sure I want to close it.

No, I know I don't want to close it. But I don't know how to walk through it, either.

And I don't know, once I'm through it, what I am supposed to do then.

I make the walk to the tower in a blur. It's through that same blur that I ride the elevator, and stumble into Hades' apartment. Wet noses bump my hands as three wiggly-with-excitement pups greet me. Okay, they aren't pups. They're full-on dogs, big and muscly and definitely capable of a great deal of danger. But they feel like pups to me.

"Oh! I missed you, too." I give scratches where scratches are due. Then I stand, and with my heart slamming behind the cage of my chest, make my way into the kitchen.

I find Hades as I found him yesterday, with takeout waiting.

Nerves rattle inside my body and I do my best to swallow them down before I speak. "You've gotta stop doing that."

"Doing what?" Hades asks, pulling a dish from a brown bag.

"Buying dinner." I throw my hand at the offending bag. "You're paying me to make it."

His lips twitch into a smile that never fully forms. "Say thank you, Persephone."

God, he's sexy when he makes commands. *Wait, what?*

Did I just see his lips twitch? Again?

Why do I get the impossible sense that he's privy to some of my thoughts?

I open my mouth to allow an obedient whisper to escape. "Thank you, Hades."

He looks pleased. The idea that I've pleased him makes me feel so incredibly warm. So happy. As though I'm a moment from erupting into flames.

"Come closer," he commands again. Again, I comply and am given that pleased look that utterly delights me. I'm floored by the way that I long to please him. I've never cared about doing such things for any other man in my life.

Maybe this really is an awakening.

Whatever it is, I'm here for it.

"Relax, Persephone," Hades soothes. "I won't bite you." My sharp laugh is cut off even sharper when he adds, "Yet."

"Hades," I begin, and pause. I don't know what to say. Words won't flow.

I think I might be panicking.

What is happening to me?

Hades drops the bag to turn to me. When his hands come to either side of my face, I feel a thorn of fear bite into my strung-out heart at the possibility that he might kiss me.

He doesn't.

"Despite our earlier conversation and my vow to you, I have no intention of ravishing you right here, right now. Desire, yes. Intention, no." He softens his hard voice. "We have time, Persephone, to learn each other."

A breath of spilled nerves escapes from between trembling lips. Hades' dark eyes bounce between my mouth and my eyes. An inferno of burning desire simmers in the darkness that only serves to carve the depths of my already gaping desire for him deeper. This yawning cavern of want I feel inside the hollow depths of me is something I'm beginning to fear that even he won't be able to fill.

I feel so *foreign* to myself.

"Do you understand what I am saying to you?" Hades asks low.

I nod, even though I'm not certain that I do.

"Good." Hades releases me to focus again on the bag. When he speaks next, I feel a rush of relief pricked only by a needle of disappointment. "We'll eat, and then I must paint." As though sensing that prick of disappointment, he says, "The urge has struck and I am helpless to ignore it."

"Okay."

"I would like it if you would help me in my studio."

"Help you?" I take the dish he offers me, now piled high with food. There's no way I can eat all this. Especially not with the nerves that jump in my belly. "Help you how?"

"I use," Hades pauses. "Unconventional materials in my paint."

Sliding onto a stool, I slide into the ease of conversation as I have every other night with Hades, I ask, "What kind of unconventional materials?"

Hades smirks as he slips a seasoned carrot into his mouth. "You'll see."

TWENTY-SIX

ades

"Oh my God, Hades!" Persephone's cry is one of complete distress. Shock fills her emerald eyes and her pretty lips leech of the rose petal red that has taunted my every thought since the moment I met her.

I want to taste her mouth. *I'm so close.*

I place the blade now stained with the deep red of my blood onto the table, curling my hand into a fist as blood drips into the bowl filled with ash. She's too horrified by the fact I'm spilling my own blood to ask questions about the ash rock I'm pouring my blood into. There is a slight sizzle as my blood meets the ash.

It's a reaction, a repelling of my blood mixing with the parts of Uranus' flesh that remain, fueling the Underworld and the prisons in which I contain him and the beasts he spawned.

Persephone misses the sizzle too. Her eyes haven't left my hand as her own far more shaky hands search the table for the rag I dropped. She finds it, and I squeeze my fist of the last of my blood.

I can already feel my flesh closing. The wound sealing. The only thing the rag will do is wipe my hand clean of the blood.

She grabs my hand between her trembling ones. Prying my fingers back from the fist I've curled them into, she presses the towel down on my palm. She's trying to stay the bleed by putting pressure on the wound. The only thing she's putting pressure on is the ugly raised scar that scores across my hand.

As a God, scars are a rare thing. I wouldn't have this one at all if it weren't for the fact I've reopened this wound thousands of times over the centuries.

"I can't believe you did that." Her voice rattles. Her entire body rattles.

I've shaken her.

I find it interesting that this woman who harbours the soul of an immensely powerful Goddess is shaken by a little blood.

"It's nothing. Just a little blood."

She scoffs. "There's almost enough blood here to fill the bowl. I can't believe you're still standing."

She's being dramatic. She's adorable when she's being dramatic.

I don't tell her it's an illusion. A result when my blood mixes with the ash rock spit from the boiling river Phlegethon. I also don't tell her the bowl she's referenced isn't a bowl at all, but the skull of the creator. The first God and, in human terms, my grandfather.

"You do this every time you paint, don't you?" I want to push away the white blonde fall of her hair so that I can see her face. I want to look into gems of emerald and lose myself in them. I want to know every crevice of her human heart and etch my name into her eternal soul.

"Yes." *I want to possess her soul. I need it.*

Heat surges inside me, rising to the surface of my flesh. I feel the burn of flames in my eyes and am grateful her focus is entirely on the towel she pushes into my palm.

Today, I am God and man. In ancient times, I was all God. In ancient times, I lacked the desire to walk the realm above my own and therefore I forfeit humanity. One of the very few times I ventured from the darkness of the Underworld; I had abducted Persephone. It was the lack of human emotions, *human* empathy, that resulted in the baser instincts of the powerful God who stole her innocence and manipulated the loss of her power to flee.

In all the centuries that passed, I've never understood how she came to love me. I put her through so much. I gave her reason, time and again, to mistrust me.

"I don't understand why you would do this." I'm not sure if she's talking to me or to herself. "You don't even sell your art. Yet you spill your literal blood into your pieces." *Definitely talking to herself.* "Why?"

Oh, she does want a reply. Too bad it's not a truth I can share. Not yet.

"It is my process." It's as truthful as I can be. I don't relish the idea of outright lying to her.

"It's barbaric. Do you advertise this?" Her eyes flicker to mine. She adds a little more pressure to where she believes the wound is on my palm. "Is this why you're so popular?"

"I can't say why I am so popular. To answer your question, no. I don't advertise that I put my *literal blood* into my paintings."

Her eyes narrow, but her voice is exasperated. "You're being funny?"

"I wouldn't dare."

"You are." She looks utterly dumbfounded. "You sliced your hand so deep I'm confident we're going for stitches, and you think it's funny."

"I don't need stitches."

"Uh, I think you might, Hades, it was dee—" Her words cut off as she pulls the towel from my palm to stare in shock at the closed wound. She sputters, "H— how?"

"I told you it wasn't deep." Alright, well, that's a lie. It was deep. It's always deep.

Her eyes flicker from my palm to mine and back to the now closed wound. Her lips part, close, and part again. She whispers, "I don't understand."

I pull my palm from between her hands, even though the loss of her touch—any touch she gives me —is physically painful. The last weeks with her have been damn near torture. After centuries without her, all I want to do is lose myself inside her.

My instinct is to take her. To claim her.

I've been fighting the most basic instincts I have since the moment I saw her standing in that room, lost in my art. The war that has raged inside me is a war I fear I may soon lose.

Lifting the black-boned skull, I mix the blood and ash as Persephone grapples with the impossibility she's witnessed, desperate to shed reason on the impossible.

Finally, after a moment, she says what anyone would say. "I suppose I misjudged."

I'm thankful the wound isn't clean, still crusted with blood. If she saw a fully healed scar at this moment, I think her understanding of the world as she knows it would shatter.

Humans don't deal well with the fabric of their reality being unravelled. It tends to result in a fracturing of the brain in such a way they never fully recover.

Of course, Persephone currently possesses a human body, but she has the soul of a Goddess. I am confident that she would rise above her human fragilities—confident, but not certain. Therefore, I don't intend to test her. Not yet.

I do not wish to break her.

I say nothing as I lift my brush, and begin to swipe angrily at the enchanted canvas. I'll soon have to return to the Underworld so that I may retrieve more enchanted canvases from Hecate. Her refusal to travel to Earth grows more tiresome with every century that passes.

As I work, I feel Persephone standing close, watching. Weakness I loathe spreads like poison in my veins. My power, my *strength*, is syphoned to feed my realm. Every day, I grow weaker. I am forced to paint the prisons in which I keep the Titans more and more frequently, the wards that bind them splintering faster every year.

It's only a matter of time now that I have her back. The Underworld will remember the Goddess who breathed life into her darkness as the God remembers the Goddess who bloomed life in the wake of his rage. She will feed us all.

I don't know when I did it, but I stripped of my shirt as I always do when I paint. The touch of her small, soft hand on my shoulder bleeds power I devour deep into the marrow of my black bones.

Inhaling through my nose, flames burst in my eyes.

I blink them away before I twist on the stool I perch on. Concern paints darkness over the shining emerald of her eyes, and her rose petal lips are parted enough that I taste the sweet wine she sipped with dinner on her breath.

I fight the shudder that rolls through my body on the wake of an intense desire to claim her. Invade her.

Fuck her.

"You look—" She shakes her head and pulls her hand from my shoulder. Her brows knit. "Hades, are you well?"

At the loss of her touch, the spike of power I'd felt inside me dulls. *Interesting.*

"Will you do something for me, Persephone?"

She considers. I watch her pink tongue slip out to wet her lips. Something flares in her eyes a moment before she says, "Anything."

She doesn't know what she's saying. If she knew what I was, she wouldn't make such liberal promises.

"Come." Hooking her around the waist, I pull her between myself and the canvas dripping with shades of black, red, and gold. She looses a tiny gasp when I pull her plump behind between my legs to perch on the stool. The swell of her ass is fitted tight to my groin, and I can't help it, I harden.

"Hades."

Fuck me, when she says my name like that. *I'm already on the edge.*

"Paint with me."

Words shudder from her to fall into space that crackles with power and tension. "I can't paint."

"You can." Emotion and desire have ground my words to rough shards as they push from the depths of me. I want her like I want breath. It's more than want. Deeper than need.

Focusing, I lift her hand in mine. I abandon the brush as I dip her finger into the paint I've mixed with the ash and blood.

She gasps. "It's warm."

The only heat I can feel is the heat of her little body against mine. I move her gold dipped finger over strokes of black and red. A crown of splintered thorns and melted gold becomes the unending prison that will contain Hyperion. The glint of gold is a mockery of the sun he embodies. The sun I've stripped him of both in Tartarus and within the prisons of my art.

I continue to guide her finger over the canvas, dripping paint into swirls of torment I've ensnared within the power I've lured from the depths of her. She doesn't know it, but this prison is the strongest I've created in years. It's the first of many, because she is feeding the God she left ravaged in the wake of her loss.

For her, *from her*, he feasts.

For centuries, hunger has gnawed the flesh from my eternal soul. Tonight is the first night since the Lethe stole her from me, that I feel a bud of indulgence. The flame of burning hunger is drenched in the cool wave of her everlasting power.

Demeter tried to take her from me. She tried to steal back the power she birthed. She twisted the Fates into a web of deceit that would remain tangled and ugly for lifetimes.

She almost succeeded. Almost won.

But now that I know the game, now that I have her back, I won't be letting her go. I won't let Demeter steal her from me again.

My free hand circles her waist at the thought. My fear of losing her opens the dam of possession that has my fingers curling into the fabric that covers her belly, pulling her back flush to my chest. The scent of flowers and sun erupts like a burst of flavour on my tongue. A low growl of need rumbles from the pits of me where a ravenous God lurks.

I want to make her hunger for me in the way that I starve for her. Drawing her finger across the canvas, I drift my hand up her belly to twist the mass of white-blonde hair she's tied back in a ponytail around my fist. Tugging gently, I pull her head to the side to expose the pale flesh of her throat. Her flesh is petal soft like the inside of a freshly bloomed flower. She smells like a garden of narcissuses.

I inhale deeply. The scent of her goes to my head in a way that wine and drugs can't. I am immune to everything but her.

I dip my head, my lips a breath from her flesh as I

watch pebbles rise across her skin. Her eyes are open and on the painting we craft together. Ancient power pulses between us like magic, crackling in the air and tasting of spring.

I can't refrain a moment longer. She's stripped me of control, my need to taste her more potent than an addicts need to bow to his addiction. She is my substance.

A sharp gasp spills from between lovely lips as I drop my mouth to the soft flesh between neck and shoulder. She tastes better than I imagined. Better than I remembered. I part my lips and suck at her skin. Her head falls back against the crook of my shoulder and she shudders as I kiss her, tasting her.

Over her shoulder, I watch the soft swell of her chest rise as she sucks in a sharp breath. The tip of my tongue teases the flesh of her neck before lingering to play at the skin below her ear. She's trembling against me now, even as I continue to guide her finger across the canvas.

"Hades," she breathes my name, igniting my need for more.

Releasing her hair, my hand moves to her throat, her jaw. I guide her face to the side as I curl my body around hers until I'm able to capture her lips with mine. There is a flash of fear in her eyes, a moment of hesitation I know I should heed. I don't.

I invade her mouth like I ache to invade her body. Against my lips, hers are beautifully soft and exquisitely untouched. At first, she doesn't kiss me back. Stilled by shock or uncertainty or perhaps both, she is frozen in my arms. It does nothing to stop me as I push through the surprised part between her lips to stroke her hot tongue with mine.

She moans and I devour it. I feast on the taste and sounds of her like a starved animal. The God inside me hums his pleasure and flames roll under my flesh. I let my eyes shutter closed to hide the flames that burn there. She's not ready to see them.

Not yet.

But I burn with barely contained control.

When she shifts in my arms, her body moving slightly away from mine, a little of that control just snaps. My hand comes to her throat, fingers curling around the slender column to hold her in place. Her pulse flutters erratically under my fingertips.

She whispers my name. "Hades."

I plunge my tongue deeper into her mouth, the tenderness I do my best to cling to for her slipping.

She resists me, her hand falling from the canvas. I could force her, I know. I could have her now. Take her and claim her. Mark her...

I've done it before.

She forgave me once...

I release her. The claws of the God shredding the insides of this body that contains him.

I won't take her like that again.

Before I can do anything else, can shift to free her

from my need, she spins in my arms to throw her own around my shoulders. Shock holds me prisoner as her hands dive into my hair, gold paint surely streaking the black. Her lips crash against mine and the fire her taste ignited blazes out of control.

Gripping her thigh, I lift her leg as I pull her into my lap. I devour the breath that falls from her lips as she wraps her legs around me, the warmth of her core connecting with the hard ridge of need I feel for her.

She gasps when she feels me, tension spreading through her body. Insecurity and hesitation leech into the hot spill of her desire, cooling the flame.

I'm not about to let her push away from me now. Not out of fear.

Pushing from the stool, I stand with her in my arms. Drying paint clings to the skin of my neck as she holds me tightly. I want to carry her from my office and take her to my bedroom. I want her body in my bed, the walls to collect the sighs I fail to absorb. I want her under me, around me.

I just want her.

I take her to my desk instead. I can't recall a time in my history where my legs trembled, the waves of want surging through my body rendering me weak. As soon as her ass connects with the surface of my desk, she drops her legs from around me. She tries to straighten, but I'm already shoving closer. My hands pin the desk on either side of her as I steal a kiss from her lips.

The flavor of hesitation and innocence linger

under the taste of spring. When her hands lift to connect with either side of my face, a rumble of pleasure spills from the deep of me to echo in the vault of her. She's so deliciously warm, like the spill of the sun over the sand on a cloudless day. There is a ribbon of heat to the scent of spring that radiates from her. It comes with a nagging of familiarity I can't place, before it's washed away by the small exploration of the tip of her tongue against my lips.

I freeze for her, letting her kiss me even though I ache to take control of this moment.

I want to make her crumble for me. Shatter around me.

"Let me make you come." I'm not sure if it's a demand or plea. She doesn't seem to know either as her lovely green eyes widen. Her hands begin to fall from my face as blood rushes into her chest, her neck, her face. I catch her around the wrists, holding her hands in place. I pin her eyes with mine now that I've gotten the flames under moderate control.

"Hades, I—"

"Please, Persephone." Well, fuck, I am begging. *This is a first.* "Let me show you how good it can be."

"I'm not—I haven't—" She sucks in air, giving her head a small shake. "Hades, I've never—"

Fuck, but she's sweet. So damn sweet.

"I know." I lean in to nip the delicate skin under her jaw, soothing it with the tip of my tongue before I slide the bridge of my nose along her jawline to her ear. "Say yes, Persephone."

"God," she moans. I bury my grin in her skin. "Yes."

Yes. Her consent surges through me like wildfire. It's a thing I never took the care to possess before. I never thought it mattered. But now that I have it, I know there's nothing better. Nothing more precious.

She's offering herself to me and I—*I am honored.*

Slamming my eyes closed, I find her lips again as I release the cuff of my hands from around her wrists to grip her hips. I pull her to the edge of the desk, grinding into the warmth of her core. I've never hated the invention of clothing more than I do in this moment. I long to feel her skin. I ache to explore the slick wet of her sex.

She's going to drive me to the edge of madness.

My fingertips slip under her shirt and the sound of her breath hitching is music to my ears. I want to brand her untouched skin with my mark so that every man, every woman, human, God, nymph, and whatever else might crave her knows she belongs to me.

Sliding my lips from hers to her jaw, her head falls back and a moan topples from her lips. I nip a path down the length of her throat before soothing her skin with my tongue. She tastes like nectar and life and abundance. She is the embodiment of fertility, bestowing life into all that surrounds her.

Yet my seed never took root inside her when she was my wife. Demeter claimed it was because my seed was decayed, and even the Goddess of fertility couldn't grow life from damaged seed.

I wonder if, with her human body, I might succeed in filling her so full of my rotten seed that just one might take. Might spill roots into the earth of her. Might grow *life*.

Something more than desire swells inside me. It is a need I ache to see through with a violence I've never felt in all the years I've lived. Its focus is singular. Dangerous.

My fingers dip into the band of her shorts. Fire burns in my veins.

Tension floods her body as uncertainty sparks in her eyes, flaring caution. My fingertips graze a band of lace. A hiss escapes from between my teeth, calling pebbles of gooseflesh to the surface of every inch of her skin. My chest heaves as I stare down at her, filling with dangerous possession to claim every inch of her body, every crevice of her heart, every shard of her soul.

"Hades," she sighs my name.

Fuck it. I need this woman.

I pop the line of little gold buttons on her shorts faster than she's able to steal a breath, pushing them open to expose one pale hip and a band of blush pink lace that has my seed seeping from my tip. My hands shake with restraint. I don't want to frighten her by shredding the very clothes she wears in my haste to expose her delicate flesh to me. But I'm unpracticed in the art of denying myself that which I crave. And I crave her.

Gods, Titans, and all that came before and after, I crave this woman.

"I want you." Fire rages under my flesh, behind my eyes. Against her ear, I rumble, "I want to push inside you and never, never leave."

Her body shudders as I imagine it might when I bring her to orgasm. The idea that my words have affected her in such a way has something primal, something primitive, *something ancient*, roaring with life inside me.

"I want—" She pauses. I clench my teeth, grinding them in an effort to practice a patience I don't possess. "I'm not ready for that, Hades."

Fucking Tartarus. I want to tell her that I'll make her ready. I want to promise her that I'll flood her with a need unlike any other, so potent she won't be able to resist. I want to tug at the tiny core of darkness that dares to exist inside her—the thing buried deep in the abyss of life and golden light—that is capable of loving me. The God of Death.

I want to taunt that tiny core of darkness to the surface. I ache to push and pull at the fragile lines of right and wrong that dance inside her. To force her body beyond the consciousness of caution and hesitation, of innocence and uncertainty and fragility until she is nothing more than a being of sensation, driven by need.

I could do it. I could...

"You need to come," I say instead, nostrils flaring against the smooth skin of her throat. My eyes burn with a desperate need I won't sate. Not tonight.

She moans, but offers me no words.

I pull the lobe of her ear between my teeth. She shudders. I soothe my nip with the tip of my tongue, sucking her flesh between my lips and speaking through kisses against the hollow of her neck. "If I can't be inside you, tell me I can still make you come. Let me feel the way you shatter. Let me spill your cries and free your moans. Let me scatter the pieces of you." I kiss down the part of her shirt, over the swell of her breasts. She clings to me like I'm the only solid thing in the whole universe. "I promise I'll put all the pieces back together again." I beg, "I just need to watch you come apart for me."

"Oh my God." She can't know the way her words travel into the depths of me. The God inside me privy to her every prayer and plea.

Mine, I think. *Ours,* he growls.

I've lived too long separate from him, in a world far from my own. All the Gods and Goddesses have fallen to this easier life, concealed by the flesh of man. All the Gods except, perhaps, for Poseidon.

She makes me remember what it means to be *me*.

The urge to shift, to split from this second skin into the God of old is strong. I can't—won't.

She would never look at me the same.

This fragile human with the soul of a Goddess, the keeper of my heart and missing half of my soul, would flee me. She is the keeper of sins, the oblivious warden who commands the master of death.

She is my Queen. My mate. Mine.

Ours.

I push the cups of her bra down to expose her breasts, reveling in the shocked gasp of need and the scent of primal hunger that spills between her legs. I want to taste the honey of her, but settle for pulling the rose pink of her nipple between my lips, twirling the peaked tip with my tongue.

Hunger, dangerous and deep, hooks me in the gut. I can feel the God so close to the surface now, I fear she will see him looking back at her through the flames in my eyes if I dare let my gaze slide to hers.

With a growl of frustration and need, I pull her from the desk and spin her around. Now that she's not facing me, the God is not at danger of discovery. It's only a matter of time, I know. But she's not ready yet.

With her feet on the floor, she wobbles. I catch her with one hand around her waist as the other presses firmly into her back between her shoulders. Sharp breaths rattle in her lungs, slipping over her tongue to sound in the splitting quiet of this room. I want to fill every crevice with the melody of her moans. I want to paint the walls with images of us.

I dip my hand into the part of her shorts, fingertips toying with lace. Roughly against her ear, I murmur, "Say yes."

CHAPTER
TWENTY-SEVEN

P*ersephone*

SAY YES. His words, rough like gravel shoot splinters of need into every inch of my flesh. I am a thing of need, stripped of caution and hesitation. I am the pinnacle of hunger, but not for food. I hunger for flesh—his flesh. For the pleasures of flesh.

Sin. This is a sin.

Mom and Dad would be so disappointed.

Say yes. The echo of his words rattles inside me, warring against the teachings of my past. I still have my clothes on. I haven't really sinned. Not yet.

And still, I've never experienced a moment so driven by sensation. I've never felt so alive. As though every atom that crafts this body I possess has been crafted to respond exclusively to this man. Hades.

God, I need him. I need his touch.

Say yes. I can do this. Heat flares inside my body. His touch is like liquid fire—magma against my flesh. The print of my hands streak against the obsidian slab of his desk as I push myself back into him. He's so hot, and yet I crave this heat. My body aches for his hot touch. For the sear of his possession.

He's so tall that when I push back into him, I feel the hardness of his arousal against my spine. My head falls into the crook of his broad chest, and when he dips his head I feel the brush of his rough beard whispering over the skin of my temple.

Say yes. A whimper falls from my kiss swollen lips, and a sound of rough pleasure drips from the deep of him. I shudder against his body, my eyes sliding down to the hand that toys with my pink panties. A flutter of something quick and intense spreads in my chest at the sight. His hand is so big against me there. His skin so much darker, the burnished gold of his tan stark against the pale of my untouched skin. And his fingers —they aren't the slender fingers of a boy-man. They are thick and rough with callouses. I feel that roughness when his thumb slides up and down in the space between navel and the apex of my thighs.

Warmth floods me, spilling into my panties at the sight of his big hand against me, claiming so much of me.

I can do this. More, I want to do this. *With him.*

Say yes. Three months. I have three months with this man before I'll return home to Canada, and most likely never see him again. Three months to explore the woman I feel myself becoming with a man who has the life experience to know definitively who he is. Three months to feel everything that I want—need— to feel.

Three months...

"Say yes, Persephone." The command in his voice paired with my own inner need renders me helpless to do anything but comply.

"Yes." He looses a sound of pure male hunger, raw with need.

My knees buckle and I would have fallen to the floor if it weren't for the unending strength of his arms. One moment, I'm standing and the next his massive weight is pressing into my back, pressing me back to the desk. I ache to look at him, so watch his face as he does whatever it is he is going to do to me. But I can't see him like this. Still, there's something about the way his body covers mine against the desk, so big against my much smaller frame, that spills another burst of wet need into my panties.

He sucks in a breath as a deep rumble of pleasure sounds from him. I get a sharp moment of fear that he can smell my arousal, but I know such a thing is impossible and brush it off quickly. His hand pushes lower, beneath the band of my panties. I suck in air that sears my scorched lungs, pushing my hips back. I'm not sure if I'm trying to give him room to touch me or if I'm trying to escape him—afraid of this unknown that is to come.

Either way, I am unprepared for the hardness of his arousal that meets my butt when I do. I am even less prepared for the way he grinds his hips into mine, the pipe tenting his pants pressing into the crease of my butt still covered by my shorts.

A low growl sounds from behind me, from over me, and his other hand is suddenly shoving at my shorts. Quick fear lashes at my innocent heart as my shorts fall to the floor around my ankles. No man has ever seen me naked.

I can do this. I want to do this. I'm just afraid. *This is normal.*

"Hades," I gasp as he shoves his hips back into me. Fitting that hard pipe of arousal between my butt cheeks as he slides his hand deeper into the front of my panties to palm my sex.

He pulls in a breath through his teeth, releasing through his nose. It almost sounds like he's practicing a calming technique, and my sex clenches at the thought that I could be driving this experienced man to the edge of his control in such a way he is forced to search for calm.

Yes, I want this. I want to drive him to the edge of control. I want him crazed with desire. I want to push him.

I don't know who I am anymore. But these next three months are the perfect time to find myself, I decide.

I roll my hips back into him, delighted when he gifts me a deep groan of tortured need. I want more.

"You're so wet for me, Persephone." His voice is dark, bursting with spilled shadows as he presses his lips into the skin of my shoulder. I feel teeth slide over me as he pushes a single finger between my slit, gliding easily in the wet between my legs. He groans. "So warm."

My breath hitches and I bite down on my lip to keep the sound of pleasure and new sensation from escaping as Hades finds my clit with the pad of his finger, rolling over and around it until I am confident I'm going to die from sensation overload.

"I—" I gasp. "Hades, I can't—"

My hands slide over the surface of the desk, searching for something to hold onto—to cling to as he strokes my core with two fingers now. His finger-tips tease my entrance, sliding back to my clit, circling and stroking down again. He does this for what feels like eternity, and entirely not long enough.

When I'm gasping and panting, sweat clinging like dew on my skin, bones trembling and weak with need, Hades hooks me with an arm around my torso, under the breasts that heave with heavy breaths. He holds me against him, hot breaths spilling over my shoulder and between my breasts as he watches his hand move in my panties.

He speaks something in a language I don't know, but somehow feels familiar. It's filled with hot, dark heat that ignites my boiling blood with deeper, more persistent need.

I don't think about reservations as I spread my legs wider for him. I need something more, something deeper, though I'm not entirely certain what that something deeper is.

"Look at you," he murmurs, his voice a spill of coarse gravel against soft skin. I shiver. "So beautiful and open for me." He teases my entrance with his fingertips as his palm presses into my clit. I whimper. He sucks at the skin between shoulder and neck. When he speaks, his voice vibrates deep into the core of me. "I can't wait to be inside you. To stretch you and fill you."

His words affect me physically and instantly. A deep throb pulses in my sex. I feel achingly, agonizingly empty.

I whimper, "Please."

I don't know what I'm begging for, but I know he can give it to me.

He hums his approval, as though my begging for him is exactly the thing he wanted before he presses the tips of two fingers into my entrance. I gasp, stilling against him as he pulls free before pushing in again. He's deeper this time, stretching and filling me. He pulls out, and pushes back in until I feel him filling all of me. He roots himself deep and stays there, his thumb shifting to swirl over my clit. It's sensation overload.

I can't breathe. Air is trapped in my lungs, snared somewhere behind the cage of my ribs. Dizziness swims in my head, muddling my thoughts. The pinch of discomfort I'd felt as he pushed knuckle deep inside me is ebbing slowly away. It's swept up in the waves of a deep need for something more with every swirl of his thumb over my clit, every second his fingers remain deep in my core.

Seconds from crying out for him to move—to do anything—from screaming—Hades begins to pump his fingers in and out of me. Stars with cores of ebony burst in my vision, floating over the lids I slam closed against a pleasure that builds into a pressure I'm confident will be my undoing.

The quake begins in the core of me, subtle at first. It doesn't stay that way for long, before the tremulous shake of it threatens to split me in two. My eyes snap open as I pitch my body forward, my hands slapping out to grip the edge of the desk as Hades fucks me with two thick fingers. I'm over sensitized, trying to escape the soul-tearing pleasure that threatens to consume me by closing my legs, stopping the pump of his fingers inside my body, the swirl of his expert thumb.

But his knee is there my legs and his warning is low and dangerous. Deadly. "You will come apart for me if I have to force every drop of pleasure from you."

My eyes lock on the dry gold paint that coats my finger before my vision blurs. My head rolls back between my shoulders and I feel his big body curving around me, covering me, *consuming me*. His breath is hot and ragged. I can hear the wet sound of his fingers moving in and out of my body. I should be embarrassed, but I'm incapable of focusing on anything but the way he's making me feel. There is no room for shame in this moment. Maybe after, but not now.

"Hades," I cry his name, and he growls his approval. "Oh God—"

"Yes," he purrs darkly as something inside me crests. My fingers curl and I do my very best to escape this ripping pleasure that edges pain with the dangerous promise of a violent overtaking.

Hades seems to know what I'm doing. That I'm unable to take this—it's too much—because he commands, "Take it, Persephone. Feel it. Come for me."

It's as though his words tug on the strings that have bound a lifetime of pleasure deep within me. One moment, I'm whole and the next I simply erupt. I am untethered, rooted to this earth exclusively by the fingers he pumps inside me and the arm that bands my waist.

My ears ring as I moan. Or maybe I scream. I can't

be sure. Everything but him—his hands on me, *in me*, feels far away.

My body is shaking and I feel impossibly weak, boneless. The quick, exquisitely violent invasion of his fingers in my body slows to something decadently gentle and sweet. He's capping his possession with a taste of wonder, ensuring a craving for him lingers in the cracks of this new me he'll leave behind when he puts my pieces back into place.

He lifts me from the desk with his chest pinned to my back. Slowly, gently, he pulls his fingers from my body, his hands from my panties.

Now that he's no longer inside me, I feel an overwhelming need to hide from him. When his arm loosens from around my waist, I drop to pull my shorts back into place. I'm about to tell him that was nice and make my escape when I see what has his attention. He's holding his fingers up, his eyes locked on the two that had been inside me. Horror is a whip lash inside me as my eyes focus on the ribbons of muted red that glisten on his wet fingers.

I bled.

Oh my God, he must be disgusted.

Black eyes lift to mine as soon as the thought enters my mind. I'm struck by the feeling that he heard my thought and I can't help but wonder if perhaps I spoke it out loud.

As though in answer, Hades lifts his fingers to his mouth and sucks them clean. I'm stuck in some place between horror and new arousal as I watch him taste —*devour*—my innocence. Knots twist in my belly and I feel my jaw quite literally drop.

This man, my boss, just tasted the innocence he took from me.

How is this my life? How did I go from the God fearing, Alberta farm girl who tended flowers in her mother's shop, never having had a boyfriend or even being kissed, to being finger-fucked by my billionaire boss in another country?

I'm going to hell and right now, I'm not certain I care.

He pulls his fingers, now clean, from his mouth. A spear of something intense and hot cuts through the knots in my belly. Breath shudders from my lungs and I swear, before he blinks, I see flames in his eyes.

TWENTY-EIGHT

P*ersephone*

I CAN'T BELIEVE I'm doing this. As I rode the elevator down to the club from Hades' tower suite, tugging at the short dress I found and pulled on as three pairs of curious eyes watched me, I sensed it wasn't a good idea.

But Minthe had asked me the day before—the day Hades stole my innocence with his hot touch—if I'd go out tonight. I'd told her I'd consider it, but the truth was that I'd completely forgotten. When I fled Hades' office after everything, I'd showered and fell into bed. I thought I'd toss all night long, but apparently orgasming can take a heck of a lot out of a girl, because as soon as my head hit the pillow it was lights out.

To my horror, I slept until nearly eleven the next day. When I hurried to the kitchen, expecting to find Hades as I'd found him every other Saturday since I began working for him, I found nothing but a note in black ink explaining that an emergency had come up and he wouldn't be back until late tonight, or possibly early Sunday morning.

I haven't spoken to Hades since he sucked my blood from his fingers and I bid him a freaked-out goodnight, scurrying from his office like a terrified animal in the face of a predator.

I've been mulling over everything that happened last night all day. So, when Willa texted me about joining them at the club, I figured why not? Without Hades here, it's not like I'm ditching my responsibilities. If it does nothing else, at the very least it might help to take my mind off Hades. Right?

I agreed. And then I got myself dressed up in one of the pretty little dresses Hades stocked for me in the closet in my room.

I'd felt confident and beautiful in the mirror, wrapped up in the sinful bodycon dress that hugged every dip and curve my body had to offer. In fact, I'd felt disappointed in the fact that Hades wouldn't see me in it.

With my pale hair down in beachy waves and my

makeup done with the help of a tutorial on TikTok, I felt—well, I felt good. Pretty. Confident. Sexual.

Now, I can't stop tugging the hem of my dress. I definitely don't feel like the sexual goddess I'd felt like when I stood in the mirror with the three massive pups standing sentry behind me.

Claire is the first to see me, and her mouth drops a moment before she lets out a shrill shriek. "Holy shit, girl, you look killer good!"

A hesitant smile stretches my lips. "Thanks."

Minthe leans in to loop her arm through mine. "She's right. You look amazing."

"You look great too."

"Oh, I always look good." Minthe winks.

I scan the club. "Where's Leuce?"

Minthe pouts. "Oh, she got stuck helping Hades with whatever drama came up."

I can't help it, and don't like it, but a feeling of hot jealousy bites at my insides. Leuce is with Hades right now. The beautiful woman who, without doubt, knows way more when it comes to sexual satisfaction. She's also dating the girl in front of me, I remind myself. But then the fear comes back because I've seen Minthe flirt seriously with the boys in the house.

"Are you and Leuce—um—monogamous?"

Minthe's smile is slow and promiscuous. "Why do you ask?"

"I'm just—" *Why did I ask?* "I'm just curious."

"We're life partners, there's no question about that. Me and Leuce have a very special bond. To answer your question—no, we're not monogamous. We're free to play with whoever we want to play with."

Something ugly twists in my gut. "Oh."

Minthe moves closer, her shoulders swaying as she wets her lips, eyes dragging over me. "Why, Persephone? Do you think you might like to play with me?"

"Me?" Shock spikes the pitch of my voice. "N—no."

Why am I hot? I don't understand the way Minthe makes me feel. Like I know her, but don't.

Like my body knows her. Knows her body.

I force my gaze away from Minthe as I force my thoughts from Hades with Leuce. I can't handle that. And, if I'm being honest with myself, it's not my place to handle thoughts of Hades with other women. I don't own him or have any rights to him. He can do whatever he wants with whomever her wants.

It's not like we vowed exclusivity. Hell, we hardly talked about what we were doing.

I just know that I want to do more. I want to play more. Explore more. *Feel more.*

Willa tips her head back, downing her drink. I slip from Minthe closer to the group, feeling Addison's blue eyes on me as I slide next to Willa. "What are we drinking?"

Willa's brows nearly touch her hair. "You're drinking?"

"Yep." I nod decisively. "I am tonight."

"Fuck yeah." Addison grins wide. As his eyes slide over me, I feel a wash of heat prickle at my skin. It's not the same kind of heat I feel when I'm around Hades, but it's something.

It's awareness of someone else, and it makes me feel hopeful that after these months with Hades are done and I'm forced to go home, that maybe I'll eventually find someone who makes me warm. I'm not fool enough to think I'll find someone who makes me burn the way Hades makes me burn—but warmth would be nice.

Willa orders me a drink, handing me the glass filled with a deep red liquid that is sweet and tart and instantly has a buzz going straight to my head. I finish two drinks before Willa takes my hand and pulls me onto the dance floor. I feel light and I can't stop laughing. I've never had a night like tonight, where I just let loose. Where I shove the expectations of my parents all the way down so that I'm not heavy with them. Where I'm just a girl having *fun*.

We dance until my skin is dewy with sweat before we order another drink. Addison calls for shots and I throw back two before finishing my drink. The room sways, but we stumble onto the dance floor. Minthe's high laugh has a rush of blood surging in my veins as she moves into Theodor, her hips swaying against his to the rhythm of the music. She lifts her phone and takes a selfie as Addison's hands find my hips and he pulls me back into him. Uncertainty is there and gone fast, before I'm leaning back into him. I'm not sure if I let the music move me or Addison, I only know that the feel of him behind me makes me think of Hades. Thinking of Hades when Addison's hands grip my hips makes me warm.

My head spins and my eyes flutter closed as Addison dips his head into my neck. "I'm pretty sure Minthe is taking photos of us."

"Mmm," I murmur. I'm too drunk to care.

CHAPTER
TWENTY-NINE

ades

THE RED RIVER Phlegethon boils as it rolls over the black rock of its bone bed, the magma infused with Uranus' blood as it spits bullets of fire into the souls that dare try to escape the pits of Tartarus before I've decided to release them of their damnation.

In the years following Persephone's murder, the river had thinned, the bullets it spits far less frequent than they once were.

But never had the bullets stopped. Never had the river failed to spit the rock that would cool into the ash I use for my painted prisons.

I turn to Hecate. "Looks like it's spitting rock just fine."

Hecate lifts one pale shoulder, the translucent black lace that hangs from bony limbs catching in the hot breeze that is unending when one stands so close to the border of Tartarus. "My mistake."

"Your mistake?" I repeat. I'm sure I did not hear her right. Hecate doesn't make mistakes. Her finger is on the pulse of everything within this realm, apart from the roots of Mount Olympus that stretch into the Underworld, the stony roots spreading like disease with every passing millennia.

"Oops."

Now I know I didn't hear her right. Hecate doesn't make mistakes, but she doesn't say words like oops.

I straighten my shoulders. "What's going on?"

Black lace whirls around her, caught in a wind of her own making. She enjoys standing in the heart of chaos, watchful, but never really involved.

It's interesting, considering she has her enchanted finger in all the pots.

Finally, the wind dies down and black lace falls against her pale body. "There is much going on, Hades."

Here we go. "Why don't you tell me, Hecate, why I'm here then."

"You have had her for nearly a month."

My jaw tightens. "You told me the river Phlegethon was no longer spitting ash so that you could look me in the eye when you told me how long I've had my mate for?"

"Why is she still up there, Hades?"

I feel my teeth grind behind my jaw. "It is not your place to question me, Hecate."

"Have you forgotten who helped you to carry this realm when she was stolen from us, Hades?"

"Me!" I roar. Sucking in hot breath that smells like scorched souls, I say quieter, "She was stolen from me."

"You know that's not true."

"Hecate," I warn.

She ignores it, as she is prone to do. "I have wasted away, Hades. *Look at me.*" My eyes slide over her body, once lush with curves and full of color. Now, her flesh clings to her black bones, so pale and leeched of color, I am just able to see the black of her skeleton through the thin skin that covers it. With the lace that covers her from head to foot, including the veil over her face and the mane of long black hair down her back, she is like a mirage.

Hecate continues, "I have given pieces of my very soul to keep this realm from total collapse. Evil claws at the binds of Tartarus, threatening to devour the unaware in Elysium. They will torment the souls of Asphodel Meadows, Hades, and what are you doing up there with her? Our Queen? She is the life force of this entire realm, Hades. We can't survive much longer—I can't survive much longer like this, bearing this weight. I am little more than bones and still I find the strength to enchant your canvasses."

"You know it is necessary."

Hecate's lip curls under the lace. "Bring her *home*."

I never imagined doing the right thing, giving Persephone the freedom to choose me and the Underworld, would come with such dire implications.

"I will not force her."

Hecate's black eyes shine behind the lace with enchanted smoke and danger. "I will not enchant another canvas until she is here, Hades."

"You would let the Titans free?"

Hecate shrugs her pale, thin shoulder. "Tartarus is on the brink of ruin. You have a much bigger problem than the Titans simply running amuck if Persephone is not. Brought. Home." She steps into me, her chest heaving against mine as her voice lowers, the lilt deadly. "We all know you are King of the Underworld, Hades. But she is the Queen. Before her, there was darkness here. Before her, you were the King of Death. The God of Death. After her, you became the God of After*life*. She created this realm, Hades. She birthed life here. It was from the love she had for you, the love she nurtured deep within her core that she brought life into the Underworld. It was from her womb that life sprung from the depths of this darkness, and stars burst through the everlasting obsidian of our unending night."

Her finger points to the glittering sky that has been

bright with new stars since Persephone's return to Greece—as though the stars of the realm high above the land of the Underworld can sense her nearness, and feast off the power within her nurturing womb. The piece within her that gives life to the realm of Death.

"This realm is her child, and we know what happens when infants are left without their mothers, Hades."

"They die."

Through the lace, Hecate's breath is a cool wash of darkness against my face. I clench my teeth against a shiver as she whispers, "The Underworld is dying."

And if the Underworld dies—all of the world dies.

THIRTY

 *ades*

My mood hasn't been this dark since Persephone's return in my life. I'm tense, disturbed. Hecate is right, even though I don't want her to be. The Underworld needs its Queen. I am going to have to find a way to bring Persephone home sooner than later. If I don't, the consequences very well may be catastrophic.

Hecate wasn't wrong when she said the Underworld was dying. It's *been* dying. Together with those closest to me, we've been holding the crumbling realm together, but what was so natural for Persephone to sustain is draining the eternal souls from our immortal bodies.

We can't hold on much longer, I know. And if the Underworld dies, not only do the souls waiting for their time to be reborn lose their chance, but they will be cast into an eternal nothingness. The same eternal nothingness that will claim the souls of all who pass until there are no more souls to pass. Humanity will investigate the sudden end to births, and blame it on the evil souls—*demons*, they'll cry—spilled from the bowels of Tartarus. They will weep their confessions and pleas to a God who cannot help them. *Can't* save them.

If the Underworld dies, Tartarus will crumble. It will leak not only the evil souls bound to an eternity of punishment for their unimaginable atrocities, but it will unchain the Titans from their prisons within the blood bound paint I've sealed over an enchanted canvas. It will unchain them because my eternal life is bound to the Underworld.

I am only as immortal as the realm which I rule.

The portal opens into the basement of the Tower by design. Unknown by the people of today, my club is built over one of the greatest temples dedicated to the God of Death, now lost to time. It once disturbed me deeply, the way humans forgot their Gods and cast us into the idyllic personification of myth. The way we allowed such disrespect, too consumed by self-centered desires and Godly games to care. Now, such ignorance allows me to move unseen between this realm and the realm I rule.

Leuce smirks down at her phone screen. I don't ask and don't care, until she throws silver-grey hair over her shoulder, pinning her eyes to mine. Leuce moves with complete confidence, always has. Her unique beauty has paved the path of her self-assurance for millennia. It won't ever change. I don't want it to. Not ever.

"What?" My voice sounds dry. My mood is dark. All I want is to return to the Tower penthouse and see her. It's late, but I hope she's waiting up for me. I've never needed the taste of a woman quite like I need her right now. There is hope in a kiss. More in freely given heart. Even the most dire of circumstance can be brightened by love.

Leuce's smirk doesn't tremble as she flips the screen of her phone for me to see. The image instantly has the blood in my veins boiling hotter than the river Phlegethon. My back teeth grind and the hands I've slid into my suit pockets curl into tight fists.

Persephone is awake, all right. What she very clearly isn't doing, however, is waiting for me.

She's wearing the red dress I ordered for her. It hugs her body exactly as I imagined it would. Only, the hands on her hips aren't mine. The man who dips his lips to her neck isn't me.

What. The. Fuck?

"Who sent that?"

Leuce flips her phone back around as she drags sharp white teeth over her full bottom lip. "Minthe."

"Minthe is with her?" At the deep rage in my voice, Leuce looks up. I'm shaking.

"Don't shoot the messenger, Hades."

"Why is she allowing this?"

"Oh." Leuce shrugs. "We didn't think you'd care?"

A low growl rumbles from my chest. The God is hovering under the surface of my skin, and if Leuce isn't careful, she may just see the monster she hasn't been privy to in centuries.

She seems to sense this, because she dips her eyes. A rare submission for Leuce. She explains softly, submissively. "You've been taking your time with her, Hades. It's been weeks—weeks and nothing. You haven't told her. You haven't taken her to the Underworld."

"Why does no one understand that I am trying to give her *time*?" I roar the last word, my rage simply too much to contain.

Leuce doesn't look up. She's too smart for that. Too smart to challenge the ancient beast crafted by something much more powerful than the humans we've been pretending to be.

Her voice trembles. As do her hands. "The Underworld is in danger."

"I am aware."

"We're all in danger."

"I. Am. Aware."

Leuce slides her phone into the deep pocket of her silver slacks. She begins to lower, her bow slight but there. "We only wanted to push you. To make you jealous so that you might hurry with her."

"You wanted me to crack and steal her away to the Underworld," I say.

It's not a question, but she answers it anyway. "We hoped."

"If I kill that boy, his soul is on you." I shove from the elevator into the club, my gaze instantly finding Persephone. She's still dancing with the boy, and something akin to magma bubbles in my veins.

"Hades!" Leuce hisses, bravely grabbing my arm and hissing when she feels my heat.

I don't stop moving toward the boy who is touching *my* mate. His soul clearly remembers his dealings with Aphrodite, because like he was in ancient times, he is a master of trickery when it comes to the heart. I can see it in his sea-colored eyes. He is a seductress of women, both human and Goddess. It is the same today as it was then.

I don't know this jealousy I bear now. It was not this way in ancient times, when she stood as my mate and Queen. I had encouraged her to share her body, and she had deeply enjoyed watching me share mine. Now, I could kill the boy with the ancient soul for daring to touch what is *mine*.

Only mine.

Something hot like acid rises in my throat as I

grow near, watching the way her hips sway in his hands. I inhale sharply, trying to clear the acid—a mistake that nearly has me roaring deadly flame. With my inhale, I've scented her. She is aroused. With *his* hands on her, *she* is aroused.

I will kill him.

My hand shoots out to grab the boy by his shirt, fisting the material at his chest. Cameras on phones flash as the crowd gets loud, then quiet. I say one word, but I know he understands when he bobs his head eagerly. "Mine."

"Hades!" Persephone screams. Her hands come to my arm and she tugs at me to release my grip on Addison. The boy's chest smokes, and he plucks desperately at the shirt that covers his chest.

"You lit me on fire!" the reborn Adonis accuses, but Persephone doesn't hear him. She also doesn't seem affected by the heat that burned both Leuce and Addison as she takes my hand and pulls me to the edge of the dance floor.

Away from her friends and stumbling on her heels, she spins to me. "What the hell was that Hades?"

I sniff the air again, shocked. "Are you drunk?"

She's always so careful not to drink to intoxication.

"Oh no." She folds her arms over her chest, only making her cleavage more obvious. She shakes her head. "We're not talking about me." I want to hide her from the sight of everyone. I don't understand this jealousy that is taking over me. It's new. I don't like it. "Are you listening to me?"

"Are you drunk?" I repeat my question.

"Jesus, Hades." She rolls her eyes. "Maybe a little. I was having fun with friends since you weren't home. It's not a crime."

I lean into her, so close I can scent her cooling arousal. My anger rises along with a surge of hot jealousy. "You orgasmed in my hand last night, Persephone." Her face flares a hot shade of red. "I sucked the blood of your innocence from my fingers and tonight, I find you nearly fucking a kid on the dance floor of my club."

Her mouth drops. "I wasn't nearly fucking him. And he's not a kid."

I don't think she knows just how on edge I am.

"You were aroused," I accuse.

Her already dropped jaw drops again. "Screw you, Hades. I'm done. I quit. This isn't—this isn't worth—"

It takes me less than five seconds to throw her little body over my shoulder and step into the elevator. She thinks she's quitting. She's not leaving me, even if it means I have to steal her to the Underworld and keep her a prisoner for the rest of her eternal life.

Fucking woman.

It looks like the scheming women in my life might get what they want after all. They've woken the ancient and barbaric side of me, and now I'm not sure I can reign him in.

Fucking women.

"Put me down you—" I don't wait for whatever names she thinks to call me. I just land a quick palm to her ass, the crack of it like lightning in the small space.

Persephone screams. Rage and something else flood her little body, but she's no match for me. Not now. Not yet, before she realizes the power she's capable of.

"You don't have the right to touch me like that."

"I have every right," I growl as the doors roll open to the Tower penthouse. Three sets of stone-cold eyes glare at me, but none of the dogs move to intervene.

Before I set Persephone, kicking and screaming on her own two feet, I disable the elevator. She'll need a code to escape, and unlucky for her, she doesn't have it.

With the elevator now inactive, I set her on her on the heels that make her legs look quite literally delectable, and stalk away from her.

The sound of her finger slamming into the button has a deadly smirk tugging at my lips. It widens into a smile when she lets out a loud shriek of frustration.

"What the hell is going on, Hades?" she demands. The slap of her heels sound over the tile as she follows me into the kitchen. "You can't just keep me where I don't want to be."

She's full of shit.

I'm beyond pissed and I need air. Like I knew she

would, she follows me up the stairs to the rooftop patio. Noc, Jas, and Prim follow her.

The sky is a canvas of stars in ebony. Usually, one so close to the sky where Zeus and many of the other Gods and Goddesses have made their kingdom—the kingdom in which I am banned—would invite unsolicited visits of such Gods. Not me. I've been careful to ensure that such things would not occur, even going so far as to mock Zeus his inability to interrupt me here, so close to his own realm.

The flames that burst from the top of the tower, a shower of gold ribboned with blood red, were pulled straight from the deepest bowels of Tartarus. Not even the Gods are able to touch this flame unscathed. It is a power that is mine alone, this ability to walk in the fires unscorched. Mine and hers.

As Cerberus is of me, a companion I crafted in the beginning of my banishment to the realm of Death, when I'd been lonely and angry and filled with resentment, my dogs, as well, are immune.

I stroll to the bar, pouring wine into a glass. I can still smell her cooled arousal, the remnants of it clinging like dew to her skin.

"I'm talking to you, Hades, look at me."

If I look at her, I'm liable to whisk her away forever. I have a feeling she won't forgive me quite the same way that she did in ancient times. Something is different now. I sensed it from the very beginning.

If I take her, force her, I might succeed in capturing

her body, but I will lose the ability to ever possess her heart. And her soul? It would be lost to me. There, but eternally out of reach.

I can imagine no greater torment. To be so close to the one thing that I require to survive, and live with the knowledge that she could be stolen from me at any moment.

It would drive me to madness. I know, I'm nearly there already and it's only been weeks. I can only imagine the effect that years of this would have on me. On her. The love I desperately want from her would sour with loathing, darken with hate.

The very thought has my teeth grinding, hands shaking.

"I am a jealous man, Persephone," I hear myself admit.

She stops moving closer, and I turn to look at her. She sways on her heels, the drink she consumed obviously having gone to her head. Her voice softens. "I was only dancing with him."

I roll my lips. Then I'm closing the distance between us, towering over her. Her breaths increase, goosebumps pricking her flesh. Tension leeches from my words as I growl, "You were aroused. I could smell it on you." Her lovely green eyes widen. "I can still smell it on you." My lip curls as I inhale again, as though to prove my point. "And I can smell him on you too."

As I make to turn away, the fire under my flesh

flaring again, Persephone catches me. "Don't—don't walk away from me."

Does she truly not know how close to snapping I am?

How dangerous this moment is for her? For me? Our future? I could ruin it all this very moment.

I shutter my eyes, not allowing myself to breathe, lest I scent him on her.

"Persephone," I warn. "I am trying to keep from doing something I will regret."

"I don't understand, Hades."

She truly sounds confused. How can that be?

She gasps when I open my eyes. I know she can see the flames there in the depths of the black. It's the first time I do nothing to hide it. I want her to see a glimpse of the beast I harbour deep within the human flesh I wear. I want her to know there is more to me—to us— than she currently thinks.

I watch as it happens, the human fragility of her mind fracturing. She shakes her head, pushing away the very possible possibility of what she deeps impossible. She blinks fast, her lips parting, eyes casting downward as she stumbles back a step.

I shove the flames down, waiting. When she looks back up at me, raw confusion twists her expression. She's excusing away what she knows she saw, her human mind incapable of accepting the fact of sight when her mind is incapable of giving explanation for what she sees.

"I don't know what is happening." Her voice is

small. I suddenly feel desperate to reassure her, but I am at war with myself.

And his scent still clings to her.

I put space between us. It's necessary, even as it pains me.

"I am not a man who shares, Persephone." At least, I'm no longer a man who shares. "When I touched you last night, I thought I made it clear that you were mine."

"That's not—I mean—I'm leaving in a few months, Hades."

I almost laugh. She won't be leaving.

I pin her with my black gaze, daring her to challenge me now. "While you are here, you are mine."

I think she might argue, but she surprises me when she agrees, "Okay."

"You will not allow another man to touch you. Not at all."

"Okay."

I steal a breath—finally—and taste him on the air. I growl and her eyes widen. She wets her lips nervously, her voice painfully small as she asks, "You can really smell him on me, can't you?"

"Yes."

"How is that possible?"

When I don't reply for long moments, simply holding my breath to hold the reins of my slipping sanity, Persephone gives me a small nod. She turns away from me, looking for a moment indecisive as she stands between the door to escape and me.

She steals another glance at me, and something steels in her soft eyes. Determination, I think curiously.

And then she moves. She bends to untie the straps of her shoes first, before she reaches behind her for the zipper of her dress. She shrugs from the clingy material, letting it fall to the patio around her feet before she steps from the puddle of brilliant red in nothing but her black panties.

Blood rushes to my groin in one quick swoop, leaving my head momentarily empty of everything but her.

She's exquisite. Her pale skin, perfectly unblemished, and white-blonde hair reflects in the high silver moonlight, casting her in an ethereal glow. I watch as she sucks air into her chest, her breasts with the pebbled pink nipples expanding. I ache to taste her. To suck her breasts into my mouth, to nibble and lick and draw moans and cries from the depths of her. I long to erase his touch with mine. To banish his scent with my own.

I am a jealous God.

I watch, unable to take my eyes off her as she dips dainty fingers into the black band of her panties. Slowly, she pushes them down her legs until they are a puddle on the floor with her dress.

She is completely naked. Every inch of her delectable skin is on display for me.

She can't possibly know how dangerous this is. How very tempted I am to take this woman who is my mate, and claim all of her for my own.

I don't move, waiting, watching, for whatever she does next.

She surprises me as she moves to the edge of the pool, and dives gracefully into the blue water. I move to the edge, standing fully clothed above her as she breaks the water to look up at me.

My voice sounds rough even to me. "What are you doing?"

Her eyes drag the length of me, landing on my erection and bouncing quickly back to mine. Her voice is breathy as she swims to the edge, pulling herself up to stand before me, dripping wet and lovely.

I should shutter my eyes. She is the personification of temptation and this is a test.

I can't look away from her though.

"You said you could smell another man on me," she says simply. "So, I washed him off."

THIRTY-ONE

P *ersephone*

THE WAY he looks at me like I've gifted him something grand and immense is, well, it's a little sad. He told me he didn't like something, and I respected it. Granted, I did so with a naked flare. But still.

I sense there is more to this moment with Hades than what meets the eye. Sure, he's obviously far more jealous than I anticipated. In all honesty, I hadn't thought the man had a jealous bone. I figured, like I assumed most wealthy men would, that if Hades didn't like something he'd simply throw me away.

I mean, there is a whole world full of women like me. Young, poor, impossibly starry-eyed and hopeful about the future. I am not special, so why would he think to keep me?

Even still, I'm not certain this thing between us has a life beyond the next few months. It's not like he confessed undying love for me when I told him I'd be leaving at the end of summer. In fact, he hadn't protested at all.

There is no question in my mind that this is a fling. I'll need to keep my heart securely fastened high inside the protective net so that it doesn't fall at his feet. I should really build a wall to stand behind, but I'm just not crafty like that. My heart feels everything, all the time. In the end, it might be bloody and pricked one too many times by the gentle touch of his hand, the invasion of his body into mine, his depth-less black eyes that somehow seem to touch my soul —but it is what it is. At least, even if it's dripping blood and spilling emotion, it won't be on the floor at his feet.

I lift my chin, about to speak when Hades presses his big hand into my naked belly. He's so warm and my thoughts fracture as he shoves me back from the pool. He's stalking me across the patio to the seating area, I think.

When we pass the seating area, I frown. "Where are we going?"

"You'll see."

My heart quickens. "You're not going to throw me off the balcony, are you?"

I'm only half teasing. A man as wealthy as Hades, he'd probably get away with it, though.

Hades glowers down at me. "I would never hurt you."

Something about the way he says it, I believe him. Still, I press, "You wouldn't?"

"Never."

"Why not?"

His impossibly dark eyes darken. "You are mine."

"Only for the next few months."

I don't know why I keep pressing this. Maybe it's because I'm clinging to some semblance of control when I suspect I truly have none. Maybe it's because I'm trying to press him into arguing, to insist that I give him more time. Give him more of me.

I don't know.

I just know that when he grunts a wordless reply, I am disappointed.

My net is really doing very little for my heart.

We round a wall with a walkway that looks out over a sea of endless black broken only by the stars above, and the lights so far down below they too look like stars.

The view is beautiful, and yet I am incapable of keeping my eyes on it when the room he's led me to comes into view. There is another small bar, and crafted into the stone holding up the far end of the gazebo-like structure is a fireplace currently lit with dancing flame. Between the bar and the fireplace sits a sprawling bed topped with white sheets and a thin white blanket. The view beyond the foot of the bed is a sprawling sea of stars.

The sheets are rumpled, the bed curiously unmade. I frown, my eyes landing on a door that sits in the wall, closed.

"Where does that lead?"

"My bedroom," Hades answers roughly.

My eyes tear from the door to land on his. "Your room?" I look again to the bed. "Do you—do you sleep here?"

"Most nights," he admits.

I look back to the bed. "It looks peaceful."

His lips twist, but he says nothing. His hand on my belly, however, grows heavier as he shoves me gently but firmly closer to the bed. To his bed.

When the backs of my legs connect with the structure, I am helpless to keep from falling to my back on the soft mattress. A soft, "oomph" leaves my lips as my body gives one gentle bounce before I scoot up the bed. Nerves titter inside my chest, diving into my belly and back up again as Hades stares down at me, naked in his bed. He's entirely clothed in his black-on-black suit and I can't help but think he looks a little like a devil in the dark, cast in shadows, lit only by flame and starlight.

He's so impossibly, heartrendingly handsome. I

am helpless against the throb of painful desire that clenches my core as I look up at him, every inch of my body painfully aware the path his dark gaze travels over mine.

I watch his nostrils flare as he inhales deeply, his eyes dipping to the v between my legs.

God, can he really smell my arousal? It shouldn't be possible.

He drags his eyes reluctantly to mine. Suddenly, I need to tell him. He needs to know.

"Earlier tonight with Addison," I begin and his jaw hardens. I press on, voice shaking. "You were right. I was aroused." Hades looses a growl that really has no place sounding from the chest of a man. A beast, perhaps, but man? No. "I put on that red dress and stood in the mirror, wondering how you would look at me if you saw me in it. That was when I felt the first tingle. I had a few drinks and the girls got me on the floor. Willa was dancing with Theodor and Addison— he—he danced with me. I felt nothing when he touched me. No flutter, no desire. But when I looked down and saw his hands on my hips, I imagined what it might look like—what it might feel like to have you holding me like that. My body got warm. I felt wet between my legs. I told myself maybe I could feel something for a man who wasn't you because..."

I drift off, uncertain if it's safe to admit something so intimate. Something that could expose just how vulnerable I am to this man.

Hades presses, "Because, what?"

My eyes flicker to his. Whatever I find there pulls the words from me, forcing a truth I'm not ready to tell. "You're the only man who has ever made my body warm with need. The only man who makes me hunger for touch." Shame tints my face pink. "At first, I thought it was an age kink. But there are plenty of older men in my life. None of whom I've ever felt any ounce of attraction for." I wet my lips, watching as his eyes chase the motion. "I've been trying to find proof for myself that I can feel something for someone— anyone else—even a fraction of the attraction I feel for you. I thought tonight with Addison—I hoped..."

Hades cuts me off with a firm, "Stop trying." He shrugs from his jacket, his hands making quick work of the buttons of his shirt. He bares his hard, carved-with-muscle-chest a second before he says, "You are mine, Persephone. Your desire is mine. Your body is mine. No one touches what is mine."

God, he's going to be the death of me. The butcher of my heart and tormentor of my soul. I swear, I see him flinch back in surprise as I agree softly, "Okay."

I'm helpless to refuse this man.

Hades stands still for a solid minute. I'm not even sure he's breathing as he stares down at me. His eyes are a pool of emotion too complex for me to decipher any single one. I know I'm crazy, but deep beneath the black I am certain I see flames.

He doesn't remove his pants before he plants a knee

into the bed between mine. Positioning his big body to hover above mine, he peers down into my eyes. Sincerity bleeds from his words as he tells me, "I will never harm you. Your body will never come to pain by my hands. Protecting you, providing for you, and ensuring your happiness will eternally be my primary focus."

His words are a blade slicing through the net that surrounds my heart. I grapple at the strings, desperate not to let the organ slip through the cracks. Not to let it fall.

"Hades..." I shake my head slightly, my eyes filling with emotion I'm not ready to share with him or anyone. I croak, "Kiss me."

"Tell me you understand that you are safe with me," he commands. But beneath it, I hear the plea.

I want to sob. "Please."

"Persephone." My name is soft in the deadly undercurrents of his voice.

I feel like I'm spinning out. Losing control. I am untethered, ungrounded. I need something solid to hold me in place.

I don't wait for him to kiss me. Rearing up, I cover his lips with my own, shocked for a moment by the sting of hot heat. Hades doesn't deny me, doesn't push me away. But he doesn't lower his body to cover mine even as I try my hardest, with every ounce of my strength, to pull him to me.

I feel so painfully exposed, uncovered and raw. I'm

more than naked, he's filleted me, gutted me with tender words that make this thing that can't be real feel far too tangible.

My foolish heart wants what my mind knows it can't have, and my innocent body grieves the man it's tasted and will forever crave.

"Hades, please," I beg against his lips. I don't realize I'm trembling, shaking in his arms until he sweeps one beneath my back, holding me tight. It does little to subdue the shake of my rattled soul.

I'm far too emotional, I think. I must be close to my time of the month, because this is ridiculous.

Something hot and shameful stings my eyes. Tears, I realize, too late to stop the fall.

Hades makes a noise in the back of his throat. "I don't know what to do."

"I need—" I shake my head. I don't know what's happening.

Is this what it feels like to fall?

This tearing pain and burst of helpless—what— *love?*

"Tell me, Persephone."

"I feel like I'm lost."

Hades shakes his head. He doesn't understand.

I swallow a sob. "I think—I need—I just—" *God, but my soul feels untethered. I need something to ground me. Something to hold me still. Something to tug the balloon of my heart back into place. To anchor me.*

I can say none of that. The words simply won't come.

But somehow, I don't need to. As though he has a window into my mind, into my innermost thoughts and fears, Hades simply knows.

Dropping his body to mine, he gives me his weight as his mouth takes mine in a kiss that is deeper than any I've experienced before. It's so deep, so deliciously invasive, I feel as though he's stroking my very soul with the tip of his tongue.

He hugs me to his chest, his body grinding into mine as I whimper into his kiss. Fire seeps from his skin into my own, boiling my blood and leeching into the very marrow of my veins. He is inside me and yet it's not enough. I need more. Connection. Anchoring.

Him.

Please, God, please. I'm praying, but for what, I'm not sure.

Hades makes a noise, a groan as he tears his mouth from mine to kiss a blazing path down the column of my throat, across my chest and between my breasts. He lingers there to pull one breast into the inferno of his mouth before flicking the tip of the other with his tongue. My hands are in his long hair, twisting in the waves that have fallen from the tie he wears it in.

I suck in a breath, goosebumps rising on my skin as my belly quivers under the tickle of his beard, the rough press of his burning kiss. Desire hollows me, and I cry out at the throb of empty need in my core.

God, I need him. I need him to anchor me. To fill me. Invade me, please.

A rumble of something decadently dark slithers from the deep of his chest to echo in the innermost empty parts of me. My body is alight with flame and need, my thoughts fractured with infectious want I am helpless to cast aside. To discard. It's taking over me. The only thing that matters in this moment is this man—and me. And the fact that we are two, feels universally wrong when I am certain we were made to stand as one.

I'm crazy. This makes no sense.

My mad soul could swear its jagged pieces were intended to fit into the puzzle of his.

"Hades," I cry, begging for something, but I am unsure what. "Please."

His answering groan feeds the fire he sparked inside me. My breasts feel achingly swollen; my core agonizingly empty. A sob spills from between my lips as I writhe beneath the tongue he travels over my navel. Tears leak from my eyes to fall over my temples and into my hair as my hands curl in soft sheets, searching for something—anything—to anchor me.

I don't understand why I'm feeling this tsunami of emotion, for no reason that I can fathom.

Hades sucks in a breath and moans. I think—I think he's tasting the scent of me. My arousal.

It only feeds the need I feel. My belly knots and wet heat seeps from the core of me as big hands press into the tender flesh of my inner thighs, spreading them wide. Hades drops his head between my legs, his hot tongue connecting with my clit and sucking hard, almost violently, at my sex.

In response, I throw my head into the pillows, arching my back. Air surges into my lungs with every desperate gasp I pull between my lips. I've never felt anything like this. The feel of his tongue on me *there*. His head between my legs. He sucks and pulls, uses teeth and tongue until I'm a trembling mess of pleas that tumble from the tip of my tongue into this firelit night.

The orgasm comes on faster than I can prepare for. After last night, I knew another orgasm with Hades would be intense. This one blows my first out of the water. It's like the eye of a storm, in a dark depthless sea. I can feel the waves tugging me under, pulling me deeper, and I am helpless to stop it.

It surges through me, waves crashing into the core again and again until I am limbless on the bed beneath him.

And, God, he's so beautiful. So darkly, dangerously beautiful. With his dark hair twisted back at his nape, a few thick locks fallen around is face, his gold skin and miles of muscle speaking credence to the power he houses deep within. How could I have thought that I could do this with him—and somehow keep my heart on the sideline? How could I have thought that after this with this man that my tender, untouched heart would remain the same?

I am a fool.

Because, God, I think I'm falling for him.

And it—hurts.

"Beautiful," he murmurs softly. Perched on his knees between my legs, the wide expanse of his chest, the muscles that ripple with his every movement, catching like dark diamonds in the firelight—he should frighten me. He *does* frighten me. Yet, I've never felt so safe as I do when I am vulnerable with him. *Vulnerable for him.*

I don't understand this new part of me.

"There is no sight more peaceful than watching you come apart for me." The raw emotion in his voice only gives his words more power. They invade me, swimming in my veins and hollowing out that piece of me that aches for his possession. His total claiming.

"I need you to—" A blush stains my cheeks. I writhe beneath him, my legs lifting so that I can squeeze my thighs together. I'm hoping to ease the emptiness that seems to expand inside me like a crater, as though aware his claiming wasn't complete. "Hades, I feel—"

"What do you feel?" How can a voice feel like a sentient thing with flesh both rough and yet ribboned with silk? How can he speak and leave me feeling physically caressed?

Locking my eyes with his, I give him the truth. "I feel empty. You touch me, and I feel like all the empty spaces inside me are filling—like I am becoming whole and then..."

Hades drops his hands on either side of my head, hovering above me like a dark God come to claim me for his own. The thought comes out of nowhere, but it feels entirely right here in this ancient city, with this man who feels like he very well might be an extension of my own soul.

Hades wets his lips with the tongue he used to pleasure me. My skin heats even as goosebumps pebble my flesh. His lips part. He asks, "And then?"

"And then you stop and the emptiness expands." I stare up at him, entirely naked and vulnerable beneath him, wanting to pull him to me. "It hurts a hurt I've never felt before."

The muscles in his arms flex in the firelight as he holds himself above me. "What do you think you need?"

"I—"

"I will give you anything, Persephone. Ask me to burn the world," he dares. "And I will release the flame that will claim it all, fuck Zeus and his ire." He dips his head to brush my lips with his. "Ask me for the moon, and I'll take it from the sky at the peril of the tides Poseidon commands. Speak the words and I will call for the war that will end the realms so we can begin again, new. Right."

I can't breathe. The man is wealth personified, of that there is little question. But there's something about that which he offers, so unlike a man of wealth who might promise beaches and houses, cars and diamonds. Hades, like the God of Death that is his namesake, offers something much darker.

"I just want you," I whisper, feeling the truth of those words to the very core of me. "I just want you to fill the emptiness inside me, Hades. I think—I think maybe you're the only one who can."

THIRTY-TWO

H*ades*

I MEANT it when I said I'd burn the world for her. I would. All of it. I would loose the flames of Tartarus and watch them spread across the realms, devouring life in all its forms. I spent centuries thinking Zeus got the better end of the deal, living in his golden city high above the earth. For a long while, I even envied Poseidon his command of the seas. The freedom my brothers were granted to spend with the living was a luxury I had not been awarded.

For a long time, I resented them for it. For the dank

darkness of my realm. For the pain and fear I lived within. For the souls who would come to me ruined by a painful life and meant to linger in my dark realm to heal from that life which they lived under Zeus' rule. For the evil I'd been forced to face, the sins I'd been made to endure upon judgement of a soul who would learn their lesson —who would repent—in the flamed land of Tartarus.

I resented them until her. Until Persephone.

She breathed life into the God of Death, as Hecate said, and birthed the God of After*life*.

When she'd been taken from me, I had begged Zeus to stand against Demeter. To punish her for her crime against her daughter, and against me. He'd failed me.

And I'd stewed. I'd been stewing for centuries.

But in that time, I'd come to realize that I wasn't the God who drew the short straw after all. I may not be the God who lived in the golden city of Olympus, or commanded the magical cities below the sea, but I am the God—the only God with the power to end it all. Including them.

For when the Underworld was cursed to me to rule, I became the only creature with the ability to handle the flames of Tartarus. It was my responsibility to contain them. To ensure they thrived. I had been doing both for a very, very long time.

It is not a thing that escapes me, as it escapes the other Gods who have forgotten me as I linger in the shadows of the Underworld, that I have the power to begin everything again.

Isn't that what flames are for, after all? Without flame, old life lingers to snuff out the new before it even has chance to grow roots. Without flame, the sins of the life would be left to rot the souls.

Flame is like a hot shower for the earth. It can scorch away even the vilest of dirt so that new and vibrant life can take its place. And the Gods who stood back and watched Demeter's heinous crimes against her daughter might very well be the most vile there is. After all, Zeus had been her father, and he's not acted in the aftermath of her tragic death.

If I'd been blessed with the life of a child, there is no act I would not do to see its survival. Unlike my father, and clearly my brother, I would not see my own suffer so that my life would remain as it was.

If I had planted life inside Persephone...

"Hades?" she whispers beneath me, and I blink. I don't realize I've lowered to an elbow, my forearm slipped beneath her neck as though to cradle her in my arms, beneath me. My other is holding her hip in a brutal grip that I loosen immediately.

"I'm sorry."

"Where were you?"

I cannot give her the whole truth. I am tired of not giving her the whole truth.

She is not ready for the truth. "I was thinking about someone taking you from me."

She laughs, her smile bright and innocent. Her lashes are still wet with emotion and there is a lovely pink flush to her cheeks. "No one will take me."

She says it with such confidence. "How can you be so sure?"

"Hades, no one wants me."

She's wrong. "You're wrong."

"I'm really not."

I don't want to bring up the reborn Adonis. I really don't. "Addison."

She touches a hand to my face. It's so gentle, so unlike the way most touch me, if they even dare, that for a moment I feel like I could crumble in her hand like dust.

"He doesn't want me, Hades. He might want ten minutes with my body, but me—" She shakes her head. "No."

"No one gets any minutes with your body." I can't help the way the words growl from the deep of me.

She laughs again. It's a sweet and innocent sound. It's far too light for the God of Death. There is a moment that I think I feel the heat of sunlight within the sweet warmth of her laugh. It's jarring.

Her hand moves from my face down the length of my neck to press against the ancient heart that thunders in my chest. Every beat is for her. Every single beat spells the love I feel for this woman with the soul of an ancient Goddess, my mate.

My body heats above hers with the need to sink

into her. To connect. To spell my affection in long strokes that touch her where no one has ever touched her before, or will ever touch her again. No one but me.

My body shudders with need as I fight the urge to claim what is and has always been mine.

I won't have her—won't let myself take her—until she loves me in return.

If I can give her nothing else, I can give her that.

Still, I can feel her need for me. Her body aches as my own aches, but where I ache to fill, she aches to be filled. We are the embodiment of divinities' perfection. The puzzle pieces of her most prized craft. Man and woman, fitted together as one. Mouth to mouth, heart to heart, connected. Soul mates.

I rock into her, watching her pupils expand as she pulls sharp breath into her lungs. My seed leaks into my pants from my tip, desperate to fill her.

Not yet. Not tonight.

I move my hand from her hip to the space between our bodies. Sliding two fingers between her legs, I absorb the tiny gasp she gifts me as her eyes connect with mine, surely seeing flame—a glimpse of the ancient God within the man—and not backing away. She is so soft and wet and *hot*.

I watch her face as I push two fingers into her, wishing it were another part of me, but loving this all the same. *Loving her*. Hoping to pull the curtains back on an affection she was made to feel for me.

Full rose petal pink lips part, and I am helpless to contain myself. Shifting up her body to take her mouth, the weight of my body pressing my hand so deep between her legs that I graze her core with my fingertips, I devour the sound of her moan with my kiss.

And then I make love to her with my fingers. With every thrust of my fingers between her legs, I'm given a little hitch. A small moan. A delectable cry.

I rock my body into her, kissing her, feeling all of her as she begins to unravel beneath me. When her body tightens beneath mine, I lift my head to watch as pleasure coils every muscle tight.

Her lips form an O of pleasure. A bloom of heat spills into her skin. I quicken my thrusts, my own breaths coming fast now in anticipation of her release. I can't take my eyes off her.

I want hers on me.

"Open your eyes," I command.

She obeys as she shatters around me, breaking apart beneath me with my name clinging to the sound of her lovely cry.

But I am frozen, my fingers rooted into the core of her as she spasms around me.

She had not been facing me the first time I'd made her shatter. The second, my head had been between her legs.

I don't miss it this time.

It's there and gone fast, but I see it. A flash of golden light—a beginning of all life—it's there in her eyes and then it's gone. As though her coming apart at the seams is enough to pull at the stitching that contains it, if only for a moment. *The Sun*.

But how can that be?

How can my Goddess of fertility also possess the light of all life? How can she behold the very sun?

It's impossible.

A weapon the Gods would war for.

A gift the Titans would rise again to possess.

And it just might be the secret Demeter feared so much.

A secret worth killing for.

***

THANK you so incredibly much for reading **Hades and Persephone: Keeper of Sins**. If you could consider leaving a review, even just a small sentence, those help us authors so, so much.

IF YOU'RE into getting early release news, teasers/sneak peeks, deals, potential offers to **ARC Read** upcoming releases...you can sign up for my newsletter at the link below. I'd love to have you!

https://sendfox.com/alannahcarbonneau

HADES AND PERSEPHONE: Book Two will be released very, very soon. So stay tuned!

AUTHOR'S NOTE

I have always been transfixed by the story of Hades and Persephone. The idea of being stolen away to the Underworld...or any world that isn't this one, really, is a thrilling fantasy I entertain A LOT. I mean, who doesn't?? And that's not saying that I don't love my life, because I do. It's awesome. :) I just like to escape, too.

Anyway, their story is one of many that has lived rent-free in my mind for a long time. When I was deciding which of the (thousands) of books in my mind to write, I couldn't stop thinking about these characters.

Yes, I've taken some big liberties with the story, stretching the parameters of the myth by a lot. But with every book I write in this series, the weaving of myth with ancient legend and magical beings crafted of nightly whispers, I just fall more in love. More enthralled with this story, and the characters and the mysteries that make them.

Thank you for reading, for supporting me and falling in love with these characters, this world, and all the magic that is this book, with me.

I can't wait to see you in the next book!

ALSO BY
ALANNAH CARBONNEAU

Standalone Novels

Our Dark Design

The Choice

Done & Delivered - A Christmas Romance

Pulling The Goalie - A Fake Dating Romance

Series

Gods of Myth

Hades and Persephone: Keeper of Sins

Volkov Bratva

Little Blue

Keeping Ruby

Devils Heartbreak

Devil In The Details

Deal With The Devil

Devil In The Dark

The Donnelley Brother's

Counting Stars

A Safe Surrender

Taking Chances

A Tender Touch

Creekwood Valley

The Runaway

Planting Roots

The Lasting Kind

With Every Breath

Written In The Stars

A Wish In The Wind

Teach Me

Teach Me To Live

Teach Me To Love

Teach Me To Laugh

The Demi Brother's

Enraptured

Enthralled

Wild Card

Mr. Wright Now

Mr. Wright Forever

Good Things

All Good Things

All Good Things Exposed

All Good Things Absolved

Made in the USA
Las Vegas, NV
09 January 2025

16113223R00154